THE DAY WAS PERFECT . . .

Dan and I swam together, gliding back and forth across the length of the pool like minnows, and meeting at the deep end to grab a quick hug under water.

Then I saw Dan start to tread water, his eyes not looking at me anymore. I paddled around so I could see, and what I saw suddenly made me feel as cold as the nine feet of water I was floating in.

It was Pam—and she looked prettier than she ever had . . .

Green Eyes

Suzanne Rand

BANTAM BOOKS
TORONTO · NEW YORK · LONDON · SYDNEY

RL 6, IL age 11 and up

GREEN EYES

A Bantam Book / November 1981
2nd printing . . . December 1981   5th printing . . . September 1982
3rd printing . . . February 1982   6th printing . . . October 1982
4th printing . . . April 1982   7th printing . . . June 1983
8th printing . . . December 1983

ISBN 0-553-24321-7

Published simultaneously in the United States and Canada

PRINTED IN THE UNITED STATES OF AMERICA

O   17   16   15   14   13   12   11   10   9   8

Chapter One

You know that feeling you used to get on Christmas mornings when you were a little kid, when you opened a brightly wrapped package and there inside was the present you'd been hoping against hope someone would give you but that you'd never for a minute let yourself believe you'd really receive? That's how I felt every time I saw Dan Buckley walking toward me, that's how I felt that September afternoon as I watched him walk down the school corridor to meet me after the three-thirty bell.

My heart felt as if it had suddenly expanded like a balloon to fill my whole chest, and my mouth started turning up in a happy smile. And then—snap! Just like that, it was as if my special present had turned to a lump of coal. Why? Because Dan stopped dead in his tracks to talk to Mimi Carson.

Just like that, I forgot how excited and up I'd been a minute ago. I was too busy going

1

cold all over, wondering what the two of them were talking about, wondering if Dan had just stopped to say hello and be friendly like he'd be to anyone else or if he liked Mimi more than that. But he couldn't, he just *couldn't.*

My breathing went back to normal just a minute or two later when he said goodbye to her and started heading in the direction of where he belonged. With me.

"Hey, Julie," he said in that low, husky but somehow sweet voice that made my heart turn over every time I heard it. "Been waiting long?"

"Oh, no, not at all. As a matter of fact, I just got here myself." I knew I was rushing my words out like bullets to keep him from guessing I was upset, but I couldn't help it. And I couldn't help what I heard myself saying next, either. "What were you and Mimi talking about?"

"Mimi? Oh, nothing." He shrugged, tossing his beautiful golden brown curls as if he were an adorable five-year-old and not a gorgeous six-foot-tall high-school junior. "She forgot to write down which chapters we were supposed to read for history class tomorrow. You know Mimi." He laughed. "God forbid she should do more homework than she's supposed to one night in her life." He laughed, then flung his arm around my shoulders. "C'mon, let's get out of here before it's too late to get a good table at Hodie's."

And, just as it always did, my spurt of jealousy evaporated into a cloud of contentment. Dan's arm was around my shoulders because I was his girl, and he was taking me to Hodie's because I was the girl he wanted to be with, and Mimi Carson was nobody but another girl in our class. I even felt silly for the way I'd reacted when I'd seen him stop next to her.

It had been two whole months since the first time Dan had asked me out, and I still found it hard to believe that someone as wonderful as he was could be interested in me, Julie Eaton. I don't mean I thought I was homely or boring or awful or anything like that. It's just that I'd never even begin to put myself in the same league with Pam Kershaw, who Dan had dated before me. He and Pam Kershaw had been one of the star couples at Lincoln High School since the ninth grade, when they'd first started going steady.

That was the same year I'd first gotten my huge crush on Dan. For the first few days of school, I watched him stroll through the corridors, already taller and cuter than the other boys, but I didn't think there was a chance he'd ask me out. He was too popular, too good-looking. Still, a part of me hoped he might.

One afternoon I was sitting in history class, and my teacher, Miss Stevens, was talking.

Before I knew what I was doing, I'd covered whole sheets of notepaper with his initials. And then I saw him with *her* and I knew I could forget it. After that, I kept seeing them together. I started noticing that they held hands most of the time. Then one day I noticed that she was wearing a Wilson Junior High class ring around her neck, a ring that could only be Dan's.

I was heartbroken, and the only thing that kept me going was the fact that I hadn't let anyone guess how I felt about him, not even Maryjo McMahon, my best friend. No one would believe Julie Eaton had her eye on Pam Kershaw's boyfriend.

Pam was the kind of a girl who walks into a room and suddenly makes you realize you've worn the wrong dress or that your hair isn't as clean or nicely cut as you'd thought. If you were talking to someone and Pam joined the conversation, your jokes would all of a sudden seem babyish and dumb, your tongue would feel like lead, your laugh would turn into a donkey's bray.

On top of everything, she was one of the prettiest girls I'd ever seen—and everything I wasn't. She was tall and slim without being skinny, and her hair was the natural color blond they write ads about, cascading down her back in thick curls or swinging behind her in one thick braid the color of lemon meringue. Somehow, she made me feel short and squat, even though I knew in my saner moments that five-foot-three wasn't midget size and that a hundred pounds didn't qualify me to be the fat lady at the circus. And next to Pam's golden waves, the dark auburn hair my mother was always calling "Julie's crowning glory" seemed as common and cheap as rust, and the wedge haircut that had always looked so cute and perky on me made me seem like a bad imitation of Dorothy Hamill without ice skates.

I guess you could say Pam Kershaw made me insecure. Maybe I was overdoing it a little, but there was something about her that made me feel definitely second class. The thought that Dan Buckley was her boyfriend made me push him as far out of my mind as I could for all of freshman year, a year that turned out to be less than spectacular in the dating department.

First thing sophomore year, I saw that over the summer, Dan had gotten even taller and, to me, even better looking. Second thing, I saw he was still holding hands with Pam, who was now a junior cheerleader and rumored to be already chosen for the senior squad in her junior year. So I tried to keep my eyes off him, but it wasn't easy. I mean, Dan didn't have what you'd call a low profile: for starters, he was one of the best divers on the swim team and as vice president of the sophomore class, he was on stage whenever we had a school assembly.

I guess Dan was the reason—even though I didn't even admit it to myself—that I joined the water ballet club sophomore year. I wasn't all that wild about water ballet, but as a club member, I could use the pool to practice after school, and I wanted to be prepared for swim team tryouts in my junior year. And that's the same reason I saved up the fifty-dollar membership fee to join Green Hills Swimming Pool the summer after my sophomore year. I'd pushed Dan out of my mind, but swimming had become my big thing instead.

And it was swimming that brought Dan and me together, after all, because if I hadn't joined Green Hills, I probably wouldn't have found out he was a lifeguard there. Maybe I'd even have gotten over my crush on him by the time junior year started.

Now, as we walked across the parking lot to Dan's old Chevy, I was happy again. Dan and I had been dating steadily since July. Pam Kershaw had moved away from Illinois when her father had been temporarily transferred to his company's main office in Pittsburgh, and I had everything I'd ever wanted. If only I could stop worrying that my dream come true was going to end.

Chapter Two

"Boy, it still seems like summer, doesn't it?" Dan said. "This has to be one of the hottest Septembers on record, even in Rockway. I thought last fall was a scorcher, but, whew!" Grinning, he stopped at the car door and fumbled in his jeans pocket for his car keys. "Can you hold these while I take this jacket off?" He handed me his books, which still looked shiny and new, not already worn and bounced-around-looking like mine.

Everything about Dan looked shiny and new, I thought proudly as he pulled off the denim jacket he'd been wearing over his sparkling blue oxford-cloth shirt. Even though his mom made him iron his own clothes, Dan always looked as if he'd walked out of a menswear advertisement: perfectly pressed, never a hair out of place. I looked down at my own clothes, and I saw what I'd knew I'd see. The skirt of my blue-and-white striped shirt-waist dress was as wrinkled as if it had been through a wringer, and I sneakily pressed my arms closer to my body as I realized there might be big perspiration stains forming under my arms. I'll bet Pam doesn't even sweat, I thought to myself, only half-jokingly.

"Hey, wake up!" Dan was laughing, his hands held out to take back his books. "I know I have the power to drive women mad, but you don't have to go into a trance to prove my point!"

I giggled. "It's the heat, dahling," I said in my best phony southern voice. "I do believe Ah'm comin' down with a case of the vapors, Rhett."

He opened the door on the passenger side of his old but unscarred, newly washed car. "Well, just hop in the ole farm wagon, Scarlett, honey, and we'll get some mint juleps that'll perk you up."

"Mint juleps at Hodie's?"

Dan winked as he switched on the ignition. "Will y'all settle for a root beer instead?"

Even though the temperature was still soaring close to eighty, it was a gorgeous, good-to-be-alive kind of day. The late afternoon sun was making little shimmery heat mirages all across the asphalt of the parking lot, which was almost empty just fifteen minutes after the last bell. Behind the single-story, sprawling, white-stone high school, kids were running out to the athletic fields for sports practice, and the sight of Lincoln's familiar dark red and white jerseys against the brilliant green of the mowed grass gave everything a carnival feeling.

Everything looked brighter than usual with the sun sinking slowly from mid-sky, or maybe it was just my own sunny mood that was coloring everything. The clapboard and brick houses on the road to town might have been southern plantations for all I knew, and the cornfields in the distance suddenly seemed foreign and romantic instead of like plain old farms.

Dan was in the same mood I was. That was one of the things I loved about him so much. Other boys—even my brother Dave whom I adored and who seemed so mature now that he was a sophomore at Rockway State College—acted as if they were afraid they'd seem silly or, I don't know, sissyish, if they talked about things being beautiful or their feelings or anything like that. But not Dan. He was never ashamed to let people see he was sensitive and caring, maybe because his mother was a guidance counselor at the junior high school and his father a psych professor at the college. Or maybe it was just because he knew that if *he* felt something, it couldn't be ridiculous.

"Today makes me feel as if summer's never going to end, you know?" Dan said softly as we turned onto Rockway Boulevard, the main street of our little town, which, like most of the towns in central Illinois, was mostly agricultural. The only things that set Rockway apart and made it more "cosmopolitan" (as Dan's mother put it) were the college where his dad taught and the big electronics plant where my own father was personnel supervisor and Pam Kershaw's dad had been district manager before being called to Pittsburgh.

"I'd be happy if it were summer all year round," I sighed, adding in a little voice, "After all, this was the best summer of my life."

I hadn't really been fishing for a compliment, but I felt like singing when Dan took his right hand off the steering wheel to squeeze mine for a second. "It was a great summer for me, too, Julie," he said. "But it's going to be a great autumn, too, just wait and see. And you'll make the swim team for sure. Even without me rooting for you, the coach'll snap you up in a minute."

"I hope so," I said fervently as Dan pulled into the parking area next to Hodie's, which was really just an old ramshackle diner where the kids from Lincoln High hung out. I didn't add that I was worried Dan would drop me like a hot potato if I embarrassed him by not making the team. I hated to even imagine not being chosen.

"Hey, Dan, how ya doin'?" at least ten different guys called out as we entered the air-conditioned chill of Hodie's and headed toward an empty booth in the back. I didn't even know half of them by name, but I recognized them as seniors, and my back straightened as I pulled myself up and tried to look nonchalant, knowing that their eyes were sizing me up and comparing me to Pam and that I was probably flunking the comparison miserably.

Then I heard my own name being called. It was Maryjo, who was sitting at a table in the back room that had been added on next to the counter when Hodie's expanded about five years ago. The back room was jokingly called the "Unpopularity Parlor" because the really "in" kids sat in the booths up front while those who thought of themselves as second-stringers wouldn't have dared. Not that the back room was actually for kids who weren't well-liked, since no one who wasn't at least midway popular would even have walked into Hodie's. You just knew if you were accepted enough to sit inside the ratty old diner that had been the place for Lincoln kids to hang out for so long—my mom and dad had gone there when *they* were dating in high school—or if you were a back-room person. Before I'd started going out with Dan, I'd sat at one of the wooden tables and chairs in the Parlor just as Maryjo, Connie, and Sue were now. As a matter of fact, more often than not, I'd sat with them.

"Hi, kids!" I called, pleased when my friends saw me walk in with Dan. I was nervous, but I hoped it didn't show. They had no idea that it wasn't easy being Dan's girlfriend; I was always afraid that once he really got to know me he wouldn't like me. It wasn't that I was hiding any terrible secret or anything like that. It was just that I felt that once he learned about my faults, he wouldn't be interested anymore. I wondered if everyone felt that way when they liked someone so much, but I was too embarrassed to discuss it with anyone—even Maryjo. That was almost the worst part.

Maude came by to take our order. "We'll have two mint juleps," Dan said, teasing.

Maude's wrinkled face beamed with pleasure and flushed as pink as the hankie she always wore pinned to her ice-blue uniform. "Now, Danny, I know you're putting on old Maudie, aren't you? I bet you kids want two Cokes and two Hodie burgers same as usual, right?"

"Sounds good to me, gorgeous," Dan said, winking, which made Maude's face even rosier. "How about it, Julie?"

"No, just a Coke and an order of fries for me, please. We're eating dinner early tonight," I explained to Dan when Maude had left to fill our order. "Dave's got to go to some meeting at the college about the homecoming float, so Mom said we'd eat at six-thirty. And she'll be serving my head on a platter if I spoil my appetite."

"They're planning homecoming already? How come?"

I shook my head. "No special reason. It's just that Dave's fraternity has gone real gung ho and decided they're going to win the parade float contest, come what may. So they're going to try to get the jump on all the other frat houses by starting to work on it as soon as they can."

"Good idea. I'll have to check out Lambda Psi if I go to Rockway State. Guys that determined to win sound right up my alley. Of course," he said, sounding a little sheepish, "this is all supposing I get accepted there and the fraternity shows any interest in me at all."

"Don't be silly! What school wouldn't want you, and what frat wouldn't kill to have you pledge?" The gushing tone in my voice made me cringe, and I tried to tone it down and make a joke instead. "After all, you *are* the famous Dan Buckley, star of stage, screen, and the swimming pool!"

"Me Tarzan, you Jane, right?" Dan reached across the shiny blue and green Formica and took my hand, and I could feel the warm flush of happiness rise to my cheeks, just as I could feel everyone's eyes on us. It was hard to enjoy Dan's joking because I kept wondering what were the other kids thinking. Were they thinking how lucky I was to have some-one like Dan Buckley interested in me? Or were they wondering what he could see in me after Pam Kershaw?

For the time being, I decided, bringing my Coke to my lips with my free hand, I didn't care what anybody thought. I was going to make myself not care. Stop worrying, Julie, I ordered myself. Just enjoy what's happening here and now. *Dan likes you, not Pam Kershaw. Why are you so terrified?*

Then Mimi Carson walked into Hodie's with a couple of other girls and, suddenly ignoring them, moved specifically in our direction. I knew she liked to flirt, and she looked like Dan was today's target. Sighing, I realized that at least some of my worries were real.

Chapter Three

"You guys don't mind if I join you, do you?" Mimi asked, brazen as could be, as she plopped herself down next to Dan without even waiting for an answer. She sighed too loudly for it to be for real, and from the careful way she ran her fingers through her short, dark hair, I was willing to bet she was copying something she'd seen Ali MacGraw do in a movie or something.

That's how Mimi was, always just a little too much to be true. I didn't know many girls who really liked her, and why should they? She'd never seemed the kind of person who had much interest in other girls as friends, and I'll bet that if she had more nerve and didn't mind showing up everyplace alone when she didn't have a date, she wouldn't have bothered having any friends at all. As it was, she changed bosom buddies like other people changed clothes, and the only girls who cared to hang out with her were sort of nerdy ones, who were too interested in being popular to think about how Mimi would dump them as soon as a guy paid any attention to her.

I know that sounds catty, but, honestly, that's how everyone I knew felt about her. The only girlfriend she'd ever had for any period of time was Pam Kershaw, and that was probably only because Pam felt sorry for her. I wondered how anyone could feel sorry for someone as conceited and thoughtless as Mimi Carson.

Why didn't Dan just tell her we wanted to be alone? I wondered. But when I raised my eyes from the ketchup on my empty french fry plate—which I'd been staring at fixedly, hoping Mimi would just take the hint and go away—I couldn't believe what I was seeing. There was Dan, smiling warmly as Mimi babbled on mindlessly about their history class! Oh, no, I thought, as I felt my stomach go all twisty, and my hand, which Dan had dropped like a burning ember, turn icy cold. He actually likes her! I couldn't believe it. But some of the pain of watching them was diminished by my realization that anyone—even Dan— who took Mimi seriously wasn't *that* terrific.

He must have felt my stare, for he went out of his way to include me in their conversation, as if I were some little kid who'd just stumbled into the room and interrupted the grown-ups' conversation. "Yeah, Julie, you don't know how lucky you are not to have Mr.

Pearsall for history. Mimi's right. He does seem to give out more reading assignments than anyone else."

"Oh?" I said innocently as she smiled slyly across the table as if to flaunt how she was flirting with Dan. "Who translates them for you, Mimi?" I asked sarcastically. But my crack only gave Mimi an opening.

She lowered her eyes at Dan in a way she must have thought was seductive and answered, nice as can be, "Why, Dan, of course— if I can talk him into it," she drawled. "You *will* come to my house tonight and help me with the lesson, won't you, Dan?" she wailed. "I'm just so dumb I can't make heads or tails of it."

"I can believe that," I muttered under my breath, not even daring to look at Dan. If he was falling for this little trick, I didn't want to know. But nevertheless, I couldn't help wondering if he really liked her or not.

When Dan answered, his voice sounded all strangled and strained. I couldn't tell if he was embarrassed by the brazen way Mimi was behaving or was uncomfortable because he wanted to keep their flirting away from me. All I wanted to do was leave Hodie's before I reached across the table and pulled Mimi's hair.

"Uh, I really can't tonight, Mimi," he mumbled. "Sorry."

Nothing fazed that girl, absolutely nothing.

She just giggled. "You two kids have a big date, huh?" She laughed, and I went limp with relief when Dan didn't tell her we wouldn't be together that evening. "Oh, well, maybe we can go over it together in study hall tomorrow, okay?" Her voice was growing all coy and pleading. "I really do need help if I'm going to pass the first midterm."

"Sure, Mimi," Dan said as she finally got up to leave. "You just write down any questions you have, all right? And if I can answer them, I will."

"You're an angel!" she gushed. Then she whirled away without even a goodbye to me.

Dan was shaking his head and chuckling. "She's something else, isn't she?"

"I'll say," I hissed. Then I realized other kids were looking our way. I pasted a stupid smile on my face, but I knew I wouldn't be able to keep it up much longer. "Let's go," I said softly, the words coming out dully because my lips felt so numb. "I've got to get home."

"Already?" His voice showed surprise. "It's only four-thirty. It's early."

But I was already half out of the booth and busily gathering up my books and clutch purse. "If you want to come back and sit around here all day, that's your business. But I'm ready to go!"

I was so mad I'd have just huffed out if Hodie's hadn't been filled to the rafters. As it was, I kept my books clutched to my chest to keep my hands from shaking as we threaded our way through the aisle to the cashier. And it took a real effort to grin and call goodbye to Maryjo, Connie, and Sue as if I hadn't a care in the world. Inside, I was frightened by the awful thought that it was all over for Dan and me, that as soon as we got outside, he was going to tell me he'd rather stay here—with Mimi—and I could find my own way home.

But of course he didn't. What he did, though, was almost worse. He didn't say a word or even look at me as he followed me out the front door, even though I stood at the bottom of the short flight of steps to wait and was watching his every move. He just walked right by me and headed toward the parking lot, while I hurried along behind him, trying to think of something to say.

He didn't say boo until we were in the car. Then, without turning the key in the ignition, he turned to me, his forehead creased and a confused frown on his face. "Do you want to explain what that was all about, Julie?" he asked, and his voice scared me. I mean, he didn't sound angry. His tone was even and low and sort of, well, *dead,* without any feeling, the way my dad's voice used to get when I was little and I'd done something so bad and bratty he couldn't even believe it was possible.

"What was *what* all about?" Now that he was confronting me, I tried to just keep my voice as light and bright as possible. "I just don't like Mimi Carson is all," I insisted. "You've got to admit she had a lot of nerve just to plop herself down with us uninvited. She's a pain."

He shook his head slowly. "Then why couldn't you have humored her for five minutes, Julie? I know Mimi can be sort of, well, pushy, but she's really not that bad. And if you ask me, you're the one who was pretty uptight."

"Me?" I barely recognized the little squeal that came out as my own voice. "You're taking her side against me? I can't believe it."

"I'm not taking anyone's side," he said stubbornly. "I just don't think you were very nice. What's Mimi done to you, anyway?"

"Since when have you turned into such a pal of hers?" I yelled over the sound of the engine turning over as he started the car. "Maybe you wish you were going over to her house tonight? If that's it, don't let me stop you!"

I sank back against the car cushions, my breath rasping and my eyes all hot. I was ready to cry right then and there, but I forced myself not to. To tell the truth, I realized I was waiting for him to assure me that he couldn't care less about her, to tell me how much he liked me and that I didn't have to worry about anybody else. But he didn't utter a word until we were out of town and turning into Elm Park, the suburb both our families lived in.

"First of all, Julie," he said slowly, as if he were choosing every word carefully, "if I want to go to Mimi's house, I'm perfectly free to go. We're not going steady or anything, you know," he added, in a cold way that made me shrivel up inside. "And second of all, I don't like feeling I can't even say hello to another girl without your looking at me with daggers in your eyes."

I started to protest, but he talked over me. "Do you really think I haven't noticed it just because I haven't said anything, Julie? I kept thinking you were just nervous about starting school again and that you'd get over it. But I'm starting to feel you won't be happy unless you have me under lock and key. And I can't live that way."

He braked to a stop in front of my house and put the car in park without stopping the motor. He shrugged, but he looked sad, not mean or threatening. I felt worse than ever, and my heart sank. Instead of making Dan happy, I was making him miserable. "You're just not the same girl I started swimming with at Green Hills, Julie," he said quietly. "*That's* the girl I care about. If you don't trust me—"

"Oh, but I do, Dan, I do!" I blurted, tears

coming to my eyes now. I felt so scared I didn't know what to do, but I was terrified that if I stopped talking, he'd drive off and I'd never see him again. "I do trust you, and you're right about me being nervous about school," I said lying. "I'm also scared about the swim team tryouts. I do trust you! I do! I—I'm sorry about Mimi, honest," I blurted. "She just rubbed me the wrong way for some reason." I hoped he believed me and didn't think I was acting like a jerk.

"And you don't get jealous every time I talk to someone else?" he asked with genuine concern. His voice was more normal now, and I knew somehow it would be all right.

"Oh, I guess I do," I admitted. "But," I hurried on, "it's only because I know how many girls at Lincoln are hung up on you. It's not because I don't trust you, Dan. I know I'm the luckiest girl in the world!"

His face brightened when I said that, and he even turned off the motor and slipped his arm around my shoulders. "You really mean that, Julie?"

"Really and truly, Dan!" I laughed weakly, wiping away my tears. "And I'll never say a word about Mimi Carson or anybody else," I promised, putting every ounce of conviction I could muster up into my voice.

"I like you a lot, Julie, I really do." As soon

as the words were out, Dan's lips came down on mine in the sweetest, most meaningful kiss he'd ever given me. Everything was all right again.

Chapter Four

"That you, Julie?" Mom called from the kitchen when she heard me come in.

"Sorry if I slammed the door," I yelled guiltily, biting my lip as I watched her prized porcelain figures in the hall china cabinet rattle.

"As soon as you change your clothes, dear, I could use some help in the kitchen. And when you go by Dave's room, would you tell him dinner's in an hour? We'll eat as soon as your father gets home."

"Right-o!" I took the steps two at a time, my energy surging back now that everything had turned out all right with Dan.

Dave and I had our own rooms off a little hallway at the top of the stairs, with a bathroom connecting them, while Mom and Dad's room and the main bath were off in the other direction, along with Mom's sewing room and the extra bedroom. Sharing a bathroom with a nineteen-year-old brother could be a drag.

But not as much of a drag, according to Dave, as having to wait for a sixteen-year-old kid sister to finish putting on her makeup and fixing her hair. Now I rapped on his closed door as I passed it. "Dinner in an hour, Don Juan," I chirped merrily. "Then you can go try to pick up girls with the rest of your fraternity brothers."

"Aren't you a barrel of laughs today?" Poking his head out the door, he tried to look annoyed and mature. but somehow it just didn't work; he was too cute and little-boyish, with freckles and long hair (which he just hated to hear described as strawberry blond).

"Not everyone's as grumpy as you all the time, dummy," I said smartly, even managing to do a pirouette as I reached my own doorway.

"Oh, yeah?" He leaned against the doorjamb, tall and skinny as a beanpole, and I could tell by the way he was smiling with only one side of his mouth that he was preparing a zinger. "Hope your mood remains this rosy after your boyfriend figures out what a zilch you are underneath and decides to find himself somebody foxy instead."

"Very funny," I snapped. "Move over, Steve Martin, you've got real competition in the comedy department."

"Well, *excuse* me!" Dave rolled his eyes wildly, then ducked back inside his room.

But he'd managed to get me where it hurt.

"Very funny," I muttered under my breath as I carefully closed the door behind me, controlling my impulse to slam it angrily. I hurled my books down on my old oak dresser, hating Dave for spoiling my short-lived good mood.

For some reason I felt very vulnerable lately, and even Dave's teasing, which I had been used to for years, could make me feel miserable. Usually I gave back as much as I got, but with Dan to worry about, I wasn't able to shrug off even a routine dig without losing my cool. Dave had no idea he'd taunted me with exactly the one thing I was afraid of, I thought, as I hung up my dress and took my old jeans and a faded green T-shirt off the pegs on the side of my closet.

How could Dan ever love me the way he'd loved Pam? I asked myself, sinking down on the ruffled bench in front of my little vanity table. I just looked so blah next to her! If only my eyes were wide and greener, if only my hair were a deeper auburn, if only my nose weren't quite so snub, if only—

"Darn!" I whispered to myself out loud, jumping up from in front of the mirror before I let myself get *really* depressed. I slipped on my old, scuffed pink ballet slippers and went back downstairs to help my mother cook dinner, tiptoeing past Dave's door. One thing I didn't need today was any more abuse, even if it was good-natured.

"How was school today, darling?" Mom

asked, looking up from the veal cutlets she was pounding.

"Okay." I shrugged. "Dan and I went to Hodie's afterward."

Her round, smiling face took on a stern expression—or as close as Mom could come to a really stern expression. She was really too pleasantly plump to ever look especially mad, except when she was trying to diet. Then she could look really grouchy. "I hope you didn't snack and spoil your appetite for dinner, Julie."

"For veal cutlets? No way!" I assured her, and she went back to her cutlet flattening with a satisfied expression. Veal cutlets with Mom's homemade tomato sauce were my favorite thing to eat in the world, and she knew it. "What else are we having?" I asked. "And what should I do to help?"

"We're having rice and corn on the cob," she said, not looking up from her work at the butcher-block counter. "And you can shuck the corn right now. It's in the sink. Just throw the garbage in the disposal."

The garbage disposal was my mom's latest toy. When Dad had gotten a big raise the year before, he'd splurged and redecorated and renovated the house. We'd lived there since I was nine years old, when we moved to Elm Park from the little ranch house we'd had in a subdivision on the other side of town. We'd all been crazy about the Elm Park house the instant we looked at it. Dave had gone ape over the big rec room in the basement; Dad had already started talking about how much room there was to build a little workshop in the garage; and I'd lost my heart to the big elm tree in the backyard, the perfect size for a swing dangling from its branches. And Mom had loved the big country-style kitchen, even though she wrinkled her nose a little when she checked out the appliances and the cupboards. "It's a bit long in the tooth," she said, eyeing the stained Formica and worn linoleum. "But the stove works, even though it looks as if it's left over from the Civil War, and it *would* be a treat to cook in a room that's more than two by four." She'd stood there in the kitchen for a minute, her arms folded, her head down, and we all knew that meant she was thinking and thinking hard.

"Well, Peg?" Dad had finally asked, sounding so edgy I just knew he wanted this house badly. But I also knew he would forget the whole thing if Mom said no.

"We-l-l-l," she said slowly, peering up at him. Then, in a snap, she stood up straight, a little smile curving her lips as she nodded her head briskly. "You talk to the realtors, Jim. If we can get the right deal, it's fine with me. We'll get this kitchen whipped into shape some day."

So Dad made an offer on the house, and we

were all thrilled when it was accepted. Dave immediately set up his stereo and dartboard in the rec room. Dad installed his power tools and workbench in his little hobby shop in the garage and built me a swing and hung it from the thickest branch of the elm tree. And Mom, because that's the way she was, never once complained about cooking in such a ramshackle, antique kitchen, even managing to can the jams, jellies, and chutneys that had been winning ribbons for her at the state fair since she was younger than me, ribbons she proudly displayed in shadow boxes on the wall above the refrigerator.

But now, she finally had the kitchen of her dreams, and she couldn't help but gloat over it, especially whenever one of her friends would complain about having to dump their messy garbage or how they'd give anything for a dishwasher.

We worked well together in the kitchen. Mom was the kind of cook who gave it her full concentration and didn't chatter on endlessly. Today, as she breaded the cutlets and started the rice and I shucked the corn and washed and chopped the salad fixings, I was glad she was the silent type—I was too busy talking to myself to talk to Mom.

You've got to get over this insane jealousy, Julie Eaton, or you're going to drive Dan away. He's already let you know how he feels about it.

But even as I lectured myself, the gnawing doubt wouldn't let me be. It kept after me, like a pesky mosquito that comes back no matter how many times you swat it away, and nothing I could do would stop it: Isn't Dan going to break up with you sooner or later anyhow? Sooner or later he'll find some-one else, someone smarter and more athletic and prettier.

There's no reason to feel that way, you dolt, the saner side of me spoke up. After all, he chose you in the first place, didn't he? He chose you when he could have gone out with any one of the girls hanging around Green Hills all summer. He chose *you*.

I thought about the first day Dan had talked to me. I'd spent so much energy pretending to myself that Dan didn't exist that I barely even noticed him sitting in the lifeguard's chair at the pool. And the day he picked to come up and talk to me wasn't even one of my best days. I wasn't wearing my brand-new kelly-green maillot; instead, I had on last summer's black two-piece with white trim that was getting a little dingy-looking around the edges. And one of those hideous white regulation swim caps required at the pool— the kind of thing even Raquel Welch would look ugly in.

I'd just practiced two or three jackknife dives and was pulling myself up the steel ladder at the deep end when I heard a voice close to me saying, "Nice dive! I hope you're going out for the swimming team in the fall. We can use good all-around swimmers like you."

I looked up, and there he was, sort of crouching by the side of the pool in the red trunks all the lifeguards wore, his white visor gleaming even whiter against the even, honey-colored tan of his face, his dimples flashing at me. At me! Let me tell you, I was so stunned I almost lost my grip and fell right back into the water. But somehow, I managed to look almost blasé as I pulled myself out of the pool, already tugging the swim cap off with one hand and shaking the droplets of water off my face.

"I've been planning to try out," I said when I was standing, leaning against the above-ground part of the ladder. I opened my mouth to say something else, but nothing came out. I was literally tongue-tied, and I stood there like a stick, all sorts of words whirling around in my brain while my tongue stuck to the roof of my mouth, paralyzed. Say something, you fool, I thought in a panic, something about what a nice day it is or how you're looking forward to the Fourth of July fireworks or how you're having trouble with your butterfly stroke. Anything!

But my mouth wouldn't work, and I just stood there, scuffling my bare feet against each other and wishing I'd polished my toenails, too scared and excited to even have the energy to move away.

Dan didn't seem to notice that I was acting like a moron. When I got to know him better, I understood it was because he couldn't imagine himself being intimidating to anybody. I mean, he thought of himself as just another guy. How could he guess that to me he was a Greek god?

"You're Julie Eaton, aren't you?" he asked in the same friendly, eager voice, as if we'd known each other all our lives. "I remember you from school. I'm Dan Buckley."

"Oh, I know." I barely breathed the words; they just came out sort of riding on the air as I exhaled. I concentrated on getting my voice back to normal again. "You're going to be co-captain of the swim team this year, aren't you?"

"Yeah, me and Bob Jackson. And I meant what I said about your going out for it. I've seen some of the Alton kids practicing, and I can tell already we're going to have a hard time beating them if we even make it to the semifinals. We'll need all the help we can get."

"I—I don't know if my butterfly's good enough to make the team," I admitted. "But I'm going to practice all summer and do what I can at the tryouts."

"Hey, you're in luck!" He laughed. "Butterfly's my best stroke. I'll tell you what. I'm off on Thursdays. If you want, we can meet then, and I'll coach your butterfly if you'll let me in on the secret of how you do such a perfect jackknife every single time."

"You mean it?" I asked, scarcely daring to believe Dan Buckley wanted to spend his day off with me.

"Sure." He grinned, and those dimples showed up again, like something written in invisible ink when you hold it in front of a match. "Is it a deal?"

"It sure is!"

He looked at the diver's watch on his left wrist. "I'd better get back to the old grind now. I was just coming on from my lunch break when I saw you and wanted to tell you how good you were. I've been watching you swim every day—you're good." He just stood there another second as if now it was his turn not to know what to say. "Well, see you Thursday then. About ten, okay? We'll have the pool practically to ourselves."

All I could do was nod dumbly, that's how excited I was. And that was before I even knew Pam Kershaw's family had left town!

I was on pins and needles waiting for Thursday to come, and when it finally did, I woke up at seven o'clock with my heart pounding in anticipation. I helped Mom weed the back garden and cut back the rose bushes in the front of the house, working with a vengeance just to keep my thoughts off Dan and the thrill of knowing I'd be seeing him at ten o'clock. I guess I must have seemed half-cracked, whistling furiously and clipping off roses like a whirling dervish, for I noticed Mom glancing at me strangely out of the corner of her eye more than once. When I finally yawned and said oh-so-casually, "Well, I guess I'll ride my bike over to the pool and swim a few laps now," she raised her eyebrows and asked, "Are you meeting some friends there, dear?"

"Oh, yeah, just for practice, you know," I said, thinking I sounded offhanded as could be. But from the way I raced upstairs to change into my bathing suit—the new one, the one that made me look curvy and almost slender—I know she must have guessed something was afoot.

By the time I was dressed and had thrown on cutoffs and a T-shirt over my suit, slid on my white Indian mocs, then strapped my beach bag with my towel, sunglasses, and swim cap in it to the back of my bike, I came down with such a gigantic case of cold feet, I almost decided to stay home. All of a sudden, everything I'd refused to think about loomed large in my mind. What was I going to say to him? How could I do a decent dive with his eyes following my every move? Did I really look as klutzy doing the butterfly stroke as I thought I did? Would he clutch his sides and laugh at me and tell me to forget it, that I couldn't make the swim team if I practiced for a million years and he didn't know what had ever made him think I was any good in the first place?

All those thoughts whirling through my brain made me feel feverish, and I stood in the drive to the garage straddling my bike, too dizzy and lightheaded to even peddle off toward Green Hills. If I hadn't decided the consequences of *not* showing up would be worse and that Dan would think I was a coward or undependable, I'd have raced right back up the stairs and hidden in my bed with a good romance novel all day. But I couldn't do that, and I knew it, so I took a deep breath, steeled myself, and with legs that felt like jelly, took off down the drive.

And that's how it all started with Dan and me. We didn't talk much those first few Thursdays, which was fine with me since I felt so awkward and uninteresting around him that it was all I could do to make small talk. When we did say anything, it was stuff like, "Don't forget to tuck your chin under as much as possible on this dive," or, "I think you come up out of the water too much on the downstroke." Real exciting, you know? And in the meantime, I was getting more and more hung up on him, feeling happier and sadder at the same time, glad to spend every moment I could in his company, even though I knew it had to end soon and that when he left me, it was to go out with Pam and that I'd never have a chance.

It was only after we'd met three times to practice that Dan pulled himself out of the water one day and, shaking the water off himself like a frisky puppy, said, "Whew! That's enough for me. What do you say we go over to Hodie's and grab some lunch?"

"Lunch?" I said, as if I didn't know what the word meant.

"We can take the front wheel off your bike and stow it in the back of my car," Dan said matter-of-factly, as if that were what had made me go into such a daze.

"Oh. Oh, okay," I mumbled, knowing I sounded like Miss Mental Moron but too amazed he'd asked me to lunch to know what else to say.

"And if I don't totally turn you off at lunch," Dan said, winking as we walked in the direction of the changing huts, "maybe you'll even go to the movies with me tomorrow night."

"Movies?" I whispered, sounding more and more as if I didn't understand English.

This time he noticed how weird I was acting. "Sure, you know, movies. Those funny moving pictures up on the big screen with sound that goes with them."

"I know what movies are, silly!" In spite of how confused I felt, I couldn't help but laugh at him. "It's just—"

"Just what?" he asked, sounding truly puzzled as he stopped and looked down at me, straight in the eyes.

I drew myself up to my full midget height and returned his gaze. "It's just that I don't go out with other people's boyfriends," I blurted, looking away as soon as I'd said it and wishing I could just sink through the ground and die right there instead of standing and babbling like an idiot.

But, to my surprise, Dan didn't laugh or make fun of me. He just said, his voice rising in surprise, "You mean you didn't know Pam and I broke up and she moved to Pittsburgh with her folks?"

"You what?" I practically screeched in shock.

"Sure, at the end of the school term." He shrugged as if it were no big thing that he was actually available. "I just figured everybody knew it."

The dull weight I'd been carrying around ever since that first day Dan had talked to me about diving suddenly just picked itself right up and flew away. I felt light as a bird, and if I'd have been alone, I even might have jumped for joy. "In that case," I said with as much casual dignity as I could muster, "I'd love to go to the movies with you."

I wheeled around then and headed to the girls' changing room, not wanting him to see the flush I could feel rising to my cheeks or the thudding of my heart through my bathing suit. But when I was almost to the door, I heard him call and turned around.

"Hey, Julie, if you thought Pam was still around, why'd you think I kept asking you to practice with me?" His laughter was loud now, but it was like music to my ears. "Boy, don't tell me you think I care about swimming *that* much!"

Giggling, I dashed in to change. And that's how it all began.

Chapter Five

I was busy setting the round maple table in the dining room when the front door opened and closed and Dad's deep voice called, "Hi, I'm home."

Mom came out to meet him and kiss him hello as she always did, wiping her hands on her apron and patting her hair into place as she walked through the dining room. I heard the hall closet open and shut as Dad hung up his suit jacket, then Mom's lilting, musical voice chiming, "Don't get too comfy with your paper, Jim. You know tonight's the night Dave's got to be on campus. We'll be eating in about ten minutes."

Dad chuckled. "That'll give me just enough time to find out what's going on in the big city."

As Mom came back through on her way to the kitchen to serve the food, I heard the crackle of paper and knew Dad was making himself comfortable as he did each and every day after work, sitting in the big, overstuffed armchair by the fieldstone fireplace reading the Chicago paper. Mornings, the *Rockway Gazette* was delivered to the front door, but evenings, Dad never failed to stop at the newsstand on the way home to get at least one of the metropolitan dailies. And he'd always encouraged Dave and me to read them, too. "Not just the funnies, kids," he'd say. "It never hurts to know what's going on in the world."

Once I told him lazily, "Dad, we learn all this stuff on the TV news anyhow."

"Television isn't the same," he'd said seriously, his voice firm. "I don't want my children growing up not knowing the pleasure of reading. Goodness knows where we'd all be today if I hadn't enjoyed reading enough to educate myself."

Dad rarely got that lecturish tone in his voice, but I knew that one thing he took pretty darned seriously was a good education. His own parents, who died so long ago I couldn't remember them, had been poor dirt farmers when suburbs like Elm Park didn't even exist and Rockway was just a sleepy little farming village. Dad had quit high school in the tenth grade to help support them, and only through working on his own to keep up his studies had he finally gone back and graduated, then saved money to take a management course in Chicago.

Mom was always strict about how late we stayed out or if we ate enough vegetables and finished our orange juice in the mornings, but it was Dad who'd always disciplined us where schoolwork was concerned, and anytime Dave or I goofed off in our studies, we knew we were disappointing him. Since we considered Dad just about perfect, we probably worked harder than we would have otherwise, because his pride in us when we did well made us feel so good and his disappointment if we got a bad grade (even though he'd never yell or make us feel stupid) always made us all the more determined to do better.

Now, as I finished setting the table and carefully lit the long white candles in the blue-and-white Wedgewood candleholders Dad had given Mom last year for their twenty-first wedding anniversary, I could hear his contented hmmms and ahs coming from the other side of the entrance hall as he scanned the paper. From the kitchen came the sound of Mom's cheerful, if off-key, humming of "Some Enchanted Evening." And from upstairs I could just barely hear the bass line of one of Dave's old Beatles albums.

Everyone's happy in their own little world around here but me, I thought resentfully. But I really couldn't make myself feel mad at the rest of the family. After all, I was the one who should be on cloud nine and if I was determined to mope and worry instead of being thankful for whatever interest in me Dan had, I knew it wasn't anybody else's fault, certainly not Mom's and Dad's or Dave's.

"Call your brother and father, would you please, Julie?" Mom asked, setting down a platter of veal cutlets on the black wrought-iron trivet I'd set in the middle of the table. "Then you can bring in the salad bowls while I dish up the rest of this hot stuff."

All through dinner, I barely paid attention to the conversation (which was mostly Dave bragging about how his fraternity house was going to have the best homecoming float in the entire history of Rockway State) because part of me was keyed up listening for the telephone on the kitchen wall to ring, even though I didn't actually expect it to. Mom and Dad would allow me to date Dan only on weekends and one night during the week, unless it was a school event or an after-school date, and since we'd already had a late study night together at his house once this week and were planning to go to Sue Hobson's party Saturday, there was no reason to expect him to call. I just wished he would, to prove once and for all he wasn't mad at me.

When the telephone finally did start ringing, I almost popped straight out of my seat, but Mom, who was closest to the kitchen, held up a hand. "You finish your dinner, dear. I'll get it."

And when I heard her muted tones coming from the other side of the swinging door, I guessed with a sinking heart it wasn't for me.

"Jim," she said, poking her head around the edge of the doorway, "it's Betty Morrison. She and Herb want to know if we feel like a few rubbers of bridge later on. Since we're eating so early, it might be nice to drop over there for a few hours."

"Sounds great." Dad looked up from the second veal cutlet he was finishing and grinned. "As long as they're prepared to be beaten, that is."

Mom lightly tsk-tsked at him, then we could all hear her saying, "Jim says he'd love to, Betty. Why don't we stop by at about nine o'clock?"

"You shouldn't be so smug about your bridge game," she told Dad in mock disgust when she'd sat down. "Betty says she and Jim absolutely slayed the Walkers last week."

"Hurrumph!" Dad pushed back his chair and picked up his dishes to carry them into the kitchen. "One of these days your friends are going to have to recognize me as the bridge genius I am."

As soon as the kitchen door had swung shut behind him, Mom made a face at Dave and me. "Modesty was never one of your father's strong points. Not, of course," she added quickly as he came back into the room, "that he isn't the best player in the neighborhood. Why, I'll bet he'd be championship level if he had the time to play that much."

"That, I believe, is what they call damning me with faint praise," Dad quipped. "But what's even more important than my dynamite bridge technique right now is, what's for dessert?"

I just picked at my slice of hot apple pie, feeling more forlorn by the minute. I didn't look forward to sitting home alone all night without even Dave or my folks to watch TV with. When the phone finally rang and Mom said it was for me, I literally leapt out of my seat.

It was Maryjo, and if she'd have been next to me instead of down the street, I'd have kissed her, that's how happy I was to hear her voice. "Want to come over here to watch TV? My folks went out to dinner, and I know they'll be back late, so we'll have the place to ourselves."

"Sure. That sounds great," I said quickly. "How about math homework? You do yours yet?"

"Are you kidding? I never do math till the last minute if I can help it. Why don't you bring your book with you, and we'll do it together?"

"Done! I'll be over in half an hour—unless Mom says no. But I know she won't since they're all going out anyway."

"Okay. And wait till you taste this new ice cream my mom got at the store. It's full of fudge and caramel *and* nuts. Obscene!"

"I thought you were on a diet, Maryjo," I reminded her. Not that she was fat or anything. Maryjo was one of those girls who was always just a little bit overweight and insisted on buying clothes a size too small because she was going to lose enough weight to fit into them and instead ending up selling them all to her friends at a discount after they'd hung in her closet with the tags still on them for two months.

"I've been starving myself lately!" she wailed dramatically. "Anyway, ice cream's only fattening if you gorge yourself. We'll have little bitsy portions. Look, if you don't call, I'll see you when you get here."

Mom said it was all right for me to go as long as I was home by ten o'clock, so I scooted upstairs to pull on a sweater and brush my teeth. I felt better just having something to do besides sitting around by myself. Besides, Maryjo and I always had a good time, and I'd known her for so long we never felt funny just sitting around in front of the boob tube together. That's what's nice about girlfriends, you know? You can let yourself go and be yourself around them, without always worrying whether you're being boring.

One thing did worry me, though, as I walked through the arch formed by streetlights and trees to Maryjo's house, which was seven doors down on the other side of the street. Had she noticed Dan and I were on the verge of a fight at Hodie's?

I hoped not, and I could have just kicked myself for being less than cool about Mimi Carson. I mean, it's not as if I actually *lied* to Maryjo, but she looked up to me because I was going out with such a catch as Dan Buckley, while the only guy she'd dated much since ninth grade was Tim Matthews (and even she admitted she didn't know why she kept seeing him since if she hadn't started hearing bells whenever he kissed her by now, she probably never would). So I just didn't let her know that I was probably more amazed than she was at Dan's interest in me. Instead, I tried to act like it wasn't such a big thing. A girl's got to have a few secrets even from her friends, and I didn't want anyone, not even Maryjo, giving me lots of sympathy if Dan dumped me.

Please don't let her have seen I was uptight, I prayed as I walked up the little winding footpath that led to the McMahons' house, a sprawling two-story fieldstone a lot like ours. Maybe, I thought hopefully, I could just avoid the subject of Dan completely, even if it meant gobbling down ten bowls of ice cream.

Fat chance! The minute Maryjo had answered the door after my knock, her round freckled face looked questioningly at me from under her shaggy, dark blond hair. And wouldn't you just know it? The first words out of her mouth were, "What were you and Dan so uptight about this afternoon, anyway, Julie? Boy, I've never seen either of you look so mad!"

"Mad?" I made my eyes go as wide as hers, but in amazement and not nosiness. I shook my head as if I couldn't imagine what she was talking about. But I'm not used to lying, so I had to avoid her eyes and walk into the living room in front of her, not even looking in her direction as I flopped down on the couch and started flipping through the *TV Guide.* "I certainly wasn't mad. Oh—I know," I said as if it had just come into my mind, "it's probably that Dan was ticked off 'cause I had to go home early."

"Oh?" She sounded disappointed, almost as if she'd wished we *had* been fighting.

"Dave had some fraternity meeting tonight, so we had dinner earlier than usual," I told her, hoping she'd take the hint and switch the subject.

"Boy, it beats me!" She sank back against the cushions, and I could feel her eyes on me, like high-powered microscopes. "Connie, Sue, and I were sure Dan was jealous over the way Gary Howe was watching every move you made."

Well, that really perked me up. "Who in the world is Gary Howe?" I asked, dumbfounded.

I'm serious. I didn't even know who the guy was. Now it was my turn to stare at Maryjo. I couldn't help but wonder if she was just making it all up and putting me on.

"Maybe you didn't see him. He was sitting in back of you. But Dan could see him, and it looked to me as if he didn't care for the way Gary Howe was eyeing you one bit!"

"How could you tell?" I asked, still trying to puzzle out whether Dan could possibly have been uptight over some other guy looking at me.

"Well, I couldn't, not really," she admitted. "But as soon as you two got up and stormed out, not even looking at each other, we could all tell something was wrong. And we knew Mimi Carson couldn't get anyone that mad."

"Mimi?" I managed to laugh as if that were a big joke. "No way! But, wait—tell me about this Gary Howe before you turn on the TV. I want to know everything about all my admirers!"

Gary Howe, it turned out, was a senior, and neither Sue nor Connie nor Maryjo herself knew him to speak to. "But he's on Student Council and cute in a quiet sort of way," Maryjo explained. I made her tell me all about him, and when she was done, I just sat and shook my head from side to side real slowly.

"Imagine Dan being jealous!" I said, and by now, I'd almost fooled myself into believing it enough that my voice didn't sound faked. "He should know better. Why, there's no one else in all of Lincoln High I'd want to go out with besides him," I vowed truthfully.

"You've got all the luck!" Maryjo complained, but I could tell by her smile she wasn't begrudging me any of it. "I've got to admit that if Dan Buckley were flirting with me across a booth at Hodie's, I wouldn't notice Gary Howe either. Oh, well, thank goodness I've still got good old reliable Tim. And guess what? This semester he's actually starting to seem not so bad to me!" She giggled. "Maybe that's what comes of his going to his grandmother's for the whole summer."

"Ah, absence makes the heart grow fonder," I announced in a high, flutey actress-type voice, and we both collapsed in giggles.

"C'mon," Maryjo suddenly said, jumping up. "Let's forget about love for a while and concentrate on what really counts—ice cream. And if you don't admit it's the most dee-licious thing you've ever tasted, you haven't got an honest bone in your body!"

I followed her to the kitchen, but my mind wasn't on ice cream, no matter how fabulous it was. I was thinking about a new plan that had started forming as soon as Maryjo had mentioned Gary Howe. Oh, I had no idea who he was, and I knew Dan hadn't been jealous of him and that if he'd looked peeved as he followed me out of Hodie's, it was just because I'd been such a prig about Mimi.

But, I was thinking, what if Dan *were* jealous? What if all sorts of other Lincoln guys were chasing me through the halls, trying to get dates, flirting and acting as if I were really something? I was sure he'd had plenty of competition where Pam was concerned, and here I'd been, not even so much as glancing at another boy since Dan had asked me out that first time and making no secret of the fact that I was happy just to be with him.

Why, no wonder he was so smug about acting so coy with someone like Mimi! He probably thought he had me right in the palm of his hand. But all that was going to change, I decided as I licked the last bit of ice cream off my spoon and settled back against the couch cushions in the flickering light from the TV. I was going to make Dan love me if it was the last thing I did!

Chapter Six

When I looked in the closet the next morning, I wasn't sure I was cut out to be a *femme fatale.*

For one thing, all my clothes were kind of conservative. For another, when I thought about dressing up glamorously and wearing high heels to school, I almost groaned out loud at the thought of how uncomfortable I'd be all day. I finally decided to look like the old me (after all, Dan seemed to like the way I looked), but to make an effort to act more confident and sophisticated.

So the me that drank my orange juice and ate my toasted English muffin and jumped in the car with Dad for my ride to school looked exactly the same as always dressed in a blue jumpsuit I'd worn before, with the same red-and-blue flowered scarf at my neck I always wore with it and very little makeup. But I was determined to act differently.

And then Dad dropped a bombshell that

blew all thoughts of boys—even Dan—right out of my mind.

"How much money have you managed to save for that car you've been talking about getting, Julie?" he asked as we drove toward school, and I could tell by the absentminded tone of his voice he was getting at something. Whenever my father really has something on his mind, he sounds as if he's off in never-never land.

"Oh, uh, not as much as I thought I'd had," I stammered. For some reason, all anyone's got to do is ask me a direct question, and I start making excuses and feeling guilty. "I really thought I'd make more this summer," I babbled on, as if the threat of the electric chair were hanging over me, "but I had to join the pool and practice a lot to have the *ghost* of a chance of getting on the swim team. Well, but you already know that's why I could only work part-time at the Superette, don't you? I've been thinking of looking for a job on weekends, but—"

"Julie, Julie, whoa!" Dad was chuckling and shaking his head in exasperation. "I'm your father, remember? I already know your life story. And I think it's fine that you're knocking yourself out to get on the swimming team. I just asked you a simple question. How much money do you have in your savings account?"

"Five hundred dollars," I answered in a

little voice. "I guess I'll never be able to buy a car at that rate."

"The reason I asked," he went on as if I hadn't started moaning and groaning, "is that your mother and I were trying to think of something to get you for your birthday. Now, since it's not until April and you finish your driver's training in December, we figured we could make up the difference in your savings and get you a little car. Nothing exorbitant, mind you. But Norm Cavendish is buying his wife a new car for *her* birthday in March, and he asked if I knew anyone who'd be interested in the little hatchback she's driving now. It's not the latest thing—a seventy-five—but it's in good condition, and it runs okay."

He took his eyes from the road for an instant and looked my way. "What do you think?" he asked, and from the half-smile on his mouth as he tried to look uncertain, I could tell he knew darned well what I thought.

"A car of my own! I think that's the best present ever!" I leaned over and threw my arms around him as he pulled up in front of Lincoln, and gave him a big smack of a kiss on the cheek. "Oh, Daddy, Maryjo'll just die with envy!"

"From what Mr. McMahon's said, I have a feeling Maryjo's going to be getting her own wheels before you are." My father always uses dumb expressions like "wheels" when he's trying to sound with it. "But don't tell her I said anything."

"Oh, I won't. I promise. And I don't care if she gets a brand-new Cadillac, I'll still love my car best, because it'll be all mine!"

"And now, if you don't get out of *this* car, sugar, I'll be late for work."

"Yipes! There's the bell, too!" I gave him another quick kiss for good measure, then dashed up the wide front walk to the building, all thoughts of Dan writhing in jealousy replaced by pictures of me cruising by Hodie's in my little car. I hadn't even thought to ask what color it was, I remembered in dismay as I skidded through the door of my homeroom to the tune of the final bell.

Maybe my plan to raise Dan's blood pressure would have come back to me once the novelty of my upcoming car wore off (after all, how long can a girl stay ecstatic about a car she's not even going to have for another six months or so?). But when I met Dan for lunch that day, he was so cute and funny that, as usual, I was happy just to be with him.

Everything was going fine, just fine. I forced myself to push away the black cloud that descended on me whenever I saw Dan talking to another girl, and as time went on, I became more and more secure in our relationship. He did seem to care about only me, and

I knew from our talk after that day at Hodie's that I'd never again let him suspect I didn't trust him one hundred percent.

What can I say about those few months of junior year except that I was the most content I'd ever been in my life? Dan seemed to be mine, all mine, and I didn't even laugh when Maryjo said she wouldn't be a bit surprised if Dan gave me his class ring at Christmastime.

Even swimming team tryouts were a breeze. I did one graceful dive after another, always aware of Dan's eyes shining admiringly from the bleachers at the side of the pool, and I didn't even screw up my butterfly stroke. And when Coach Walker congratulated me afterward and said, "I think you're going to be a valuable addition to the team, Julie," and Dan squeezed my shoulder and whispered, "That's my girl," I could have melted on the spot. If this was all a dream, I didn't ever want to wake up.

But I woke up with a crash one evening just a week before Christmas. We were trimming the tree at home and sort of all talking at once—Dave was carrying on about the gorgeous girl he was taking to the fraternity's Christmas dance, I was telling Mom all about Lincoln's latest pool victory over Cabrini High, Mom was telling us all where to hang tinsel, and Dad was wondering whatever had happened to the delicate silver icicle ornaments he'd bought last year. The happy family at home, right? And then it happened.

"Oh, I forgot to tell you, Peg," Dad said, so casually he could never have guessed he was about to say the words that would send my whole world crashing down and shattering like the most fragile treetop star, "Ed Kershaw's being sent back. The home office hasn't been happy with his replacement, so they're flying him back at the first of the year."

Mom didn't say anything. She just murmured and separated more tinsel. It was my voice, sounding like it was coming from a very long distance, that said, "The Kershaws are coming back? Here? To Rockway?"

"Yep, first of January." Dad was too busy examining a cracked light to notice anything strange in my tone. But from the way Dave twisted his head around the branches of the evergreen and peered at me, I knew I'd sounded odd and would have bet money I'd turned white as a ghost.

"Why do you care about the Kershaws?" he asked.

"Oh, I don't. Not really." I ducked my head down and started tinseling a low branch with the concentration usually seen only during brain surgery. "I just knew Pam Kershaw from school, that's all. She was in my class."

"Well, it looks like she'll be in your class again come the new year." Dad sounded so chipper that I felt like hitting him over the head with the tree, stand and all. "It'll be good to have Ed back. He keeps things running like clockwork. He was talking to Mom again. "And all the men really like him."

Just like all the boys really like his daughter, I tortured myself. Especially one.

"Julie, if you don't stop flinging that tinsel on so violently, you're going to knock down the tree!" Mom said sharply, and I stared down at my hands. I hadn't even realized what I was doing, and now I saw I'd hurled more of the silver strands on two branches than there were on the rest of the whole tree.

"I'm just getting bored." I didn't care how sulky I sounded as I pulled off the extra tinsel and handed it to my brother. "Here, Dave, it's all yours. I'm going to read a couple of assignments and go to bed. Sorry I'm not more help."

"What's gotten into her?" I heard the irritation in Dave's voice as I started trudging up the steps to my room, so tired all of a sudden I didn't feel as if I could make it.

"Everyone gets high-strung this time of year," Mom said calmly.

"Oh, yeah?" he snorted. "Well, somebody better tell old Jittery Julie 'tis the season to be merry and all that jazz."

That was all I heard. I felt sorry enough for myself already without having to listen to my own brother putting me down.

Pam was coming back! I should have known, I thought, throwing myself on my bed and sobbing into my pillow. I should have known my peaceful life couldn't last!

By the time I calmed down, other horrible thoughts were invading my brain like enemy troops. How long had Dan known she was returning to Rockway, and why hadn't he told me? I couldn't believe he wasn't aware that she'd be back soon. Even if they weren't writing to each other (and I'd never had the nerve to try to find out if they were), Pam was surely keeping in touch with Mimi Carson. And Mimi was just the kind to let Dan know, then sit back and gloat about my being in the dark.

Don't jump to conclusions, I told myself over and over. You don't know for a fact he's still in love with Pam. You don't know that he's not happy with you. Maybe he won't give her a second glance when she's back waltzing through the corridors at good old Lincoln High like a ballerina. Maybe it's just going to be you and Dan, forever and ever.

That was the mature, collected side of me. The other part, the bigger part, was mocking me: Do you really think Dan's going to want anything to do with you after Pam's back in town? Do you really think he's going to stick with you after she snaps her fingers and tells him she wants him back? Fat chance!

I tossed and turned most of the night,

trying to put the vision of Dan and Pam to rest so I could sleep. But the two of them, holding hands, kissing, dancing at the Junior Prom, kept parading through my sleepy brain like demons in a nightmare. By the next morning, I might have been a zombie. I felt like the walking dead, and I dreaded going to school, so sure all the other kids were whispering about Pam Kershaw moving back to Rockway.

Strangely enough, the prospect of Pam's return didn't seem to be having much of an effect on anybody else at all.

I was walking toward my second period class with Maryjo and Sue when, as casually as I could, I dropped into the conversation, "By the way, did you hear Pam Kershaw's moving back?"

Sue nodded, making her aviator glasses slide down the bridge of her nose. "Sure. Alice Mayhew's all upset 'cause she's afraid they'll kick her off cheerleading next year so Pam can take her place."

"Didn't she know Pam was coming back sooner or later? Everyone but everyone knew her father's transfer was just temporary." Maryjo was trying to fix her lipstick, holding her compact mirror up at the same time she was walking and talking. She didn't seem to care much about what Pam Kershaw did. As soon as she'd put her makeup back in her purse, she turned to Sue and gave a little hiss of disgust. "Why in the world don't you get your glasses adjusted? You look like somebody's maiden aunt with them dangling half off your face all the time."

With that, they started a little friendly bickering, and between Maryjo's jibes about Sue's glasses and Sue's digs about Maryjo's famous "diet," I could tell neither of them had even considered how enormously Pam's homecoming was going to affect me. Or maybe they had more faith in Dan's loyalty to me than I did. Fools!

Still, Dan didn't say a word about Pam, and I just kept telling myself everything was okay, hoping if I said it enough, I might even believe it. But I knew I was showing the strain, and by Christmas Eve I was a basket case.

Dan had always given a big party Christmas Eve for all the kids from school, and this was the first year I'd be going as his date instead of Pam. That scared me enough. But it was also the night that Dan and I would exchange gifts. I'd bought him a cable-knit sweater in his favorite shade of green, which I knew he'd like. The big question was: would he give me his class ring the way Maryjo had predicted he would, or was he saving it for Pam's homecoming?

I could barely choke down dinner that night, even though Mom's fried chicken was as good as ever. Mom and Dad were going to a party given by one of Dad's friends at the office, and Dave was taking his girlfriend, Lois, to a party. So everybody was pretty wrapped up in their own plans for the evening. But I had the feeling, as I sat eating in my ratty old bathrobe, *still* trying to decide what to wear, that I was the only person filled with as much fear as anticipation.

"You will remember to ask Dan to get you home by eleven-thirty so we can open our gifts at midnight, won't you, Julie?" Mom asked. "If you think it might be a problem, your father and I can pick you up on our way home."

"No, no," I said quickly, snapping out of my daze at the thought of my parents showing up at the Buckleys to fetch me. "Dan says the party always breaks up by ten-thirty or eleven."

"And what do you two plan to do alone for an hour?" Dave asked, leering and rolling his eyes.

"David!" Mom's voice had a sharp edge to it. "Don't tease your sister."

"Aw, she knows I'm only kidding, Mom." Dave could still sound like a bad little boy if Mom put him in his place.

"What are you giving Lois for Christmas?" I asked, just to turn the talk from Dan and me. "I hope that old Iron Butterfly album of yours. If I have to listen to 'Inna Gadda De Vita' one more time, my eardrums will pop."

"Cute, squirt, real cute. As a matter of fact, I'm presenting her with the gift a million girls at Rockway State would be dying to get."

Even Dad looked mildly interested. "What's that? Surely not the grade you got on your last English exam."

For a second Dave's face got a sulky look, as if he was sick of being on the other end of the teasing, but I guess nothing was going to dampen his good mood, for suddenly he laughed. "Okay, Dad, I deserved that."

"Well, what *are* you giving Lois?" I asked, curiosity getting the better of me.

"My Lambda Psi pin, smarty. That's what!"

"Hey, you two kids are really serious, aren't you?" Dad gave Dave a big smile. "That's terrific, Dave!"

"Big deal," I muttered. "Hope you're not too embarrassed if she gives it back."

"Aren't you Miss Sweetness and Light tonight?" Dave asked, and from the snarl in his voice, I could tell I'd pushed him too far. "Afraid all your precious boyfriend is going to give you are your walking papers and the old heave ho?"

I pulled myself out of my chair and threw my napkin down on the table in what I hoped was disdain. "If you'll excuse me, I'll just clear the table and go get dressed," I said stiffly to my parents. "I don't feel like being an audience for this infant anymore."

"Touchy, touchy," Dave murmured, and I could hear Mom shushing him as I charged into the kitchen with an armload of dirty dishes.

I was scraping the garbage into the sink with a vengeance when Mom came in, and I could tell by the careful way she was puttering around and just sort of peering at me out of the corners of her eyes that she was about to say something. I tried to hum merrily, as if I didn't have a care in the world, but all that came out was a version of "God Rest Ye, Merry Gentlemen" that sounded like a moan.

"You go on and get ready, dear," Mom said, tying an apron around her best blue dress. "I've got plenty of time to do these."

"Are you sure you don't want help?" I asked, but I was already sidling toward the door, wanting to get away from everyone's prying eyes and concerned looks all of a sudden.

"I'm sure. But—" She hesitated, then walked over and lifted my chin up with one hand so I was forced to look into her candid blue eyes. "Is something wrong, Julie? Your brother's right, you know. You haven't been exactly flowing over with Christmas cheer this season. It's not like you to be so edgy, darling. Is it Dan?"

"Dan?" I said. "Oh, no, everything's fine with Dan." I forced a yawn. "I'm just tired, I guess. Too much excitement and all that, you know," I insisted, but my voice was so phony and bright it rang false in my own ears. "Well, I'd better get ready," I added. Then I was out of that kitchen and up the stairs as quickly as if there'd been a fire nipping at my heels. I wanted to forget my worries about Dan—not talk about them!

I'd calmed down by the time I had gotten ready and even managed to mumble, "Sorry I snapped at you before" to Dave when I passed him in the hallway as he was on his way out.

"Sure, kid, no problem," he said, giving me a big grin that made me feel like crying. He really was a great brother, and I had been acting like a creep. He ruffled my hair on his way out the door. "Have fun at your party, and I'll see you later."

"You, too!" I called after him. "And say hi to Lois for me."

Mom and Dad were in the living room, waiting to drive me to the Buckleys, and they both looked me over approvingly. "You look lovely, Julie," Mom said, standing to pat my hair back into place where Dave had mussed it up. "I've always liked you in green. It sets off your eyes so well."

"Thanks, Mom." I turned to get one more quick look at myself in the foyer mirror as I pulled my down parka out of the closet. I'd chosen my loden green wool slacks and green plaid shirt because they almost matched the sweater I was giving Dan and because I knew they showed up the golden glints in my auburn hair. I thought I looked almost as pretty as Pam Kershaw. But was *almost* good enough?

I sat in the back seat of the car, glad Dad had turned the radio on to a station playing Christmas carols so we could all sing. When Dad pulled up at the walk that led to the Buckleys' big stone house, I pasted a glazed smile on my face and sang out a cheery goodbye. But my feet were leaden as I plodded up the driveway, and even the December chill couldn't cool the heat rising in my cheeks. Tonight, I was certain, I'd find out who Dan really cared about—Pam or me—and I had a sinking feeling I'd rather not know.

Chapter Seven

When all was said and done, it wouldn't have mattered how much energy I'd used to push away the fact that Pam was coming back to Rockway, because I was reminded of it as soon as I got to the Buckleys. I was standing in the Buckleys' spacious entrance hall, putting my coat on the wooden hanger Mrs. Buckley had handed me with a quick brush of her lips on my cheek and a warm "Merry Christmas, Julie," when who should come mincing in the front door, in a skirt so tight and heels so high I wondered how she could walk, but Mimi Carson.

I fumbled to get out of the way, but I wasn't quick enough. "Hi, Julie," she said in a voice so sirupy sweet it practically dripped. "Have you heard the news? Pam Kershaw's moving back at New Year's!"

"So I heard," I said breezily, avoiding Mimi's look by handing my coat and hanger to Dan's mother.

Mimi was slipping off her jacket as I inched past her, but she wasn't too busy to lean closer and drawl in my ear, "Dan must be thrilled."

"Why don't you ask *him*?" I snapped, pushing past her and storming into the big dining room which had been decorated for the party. Plates of cookies, several cakes, and a huge bowl of punch were on the table. Still clutching my gilt-wrapped package for Dan, I stood and looked around, but Dan was nowhere to be seen.

There were a lot of kids there already, and a couple of them said hello when I walked in, but I didn't feel like talking to anyone but Dan. It seemed as if everyone was looking at me with pity in their eyes, wondering how I was taking the news about Pam. Swallowing hard, I darted into the living room, figuring I'd just slip Dan's present under the tree.

As I rounded the corner, I practically ran smack into Dan, who was standing next to the brightly lit evergreen and talking quietly to Chip Richter, a tall, athletic guy, who was the class cutup and one of Dan's best friends.

My timing couldn't have been worse—I caught only the last words out of Dan's mouth. "On the card I got, she said she was nervous about coming back in the middle of the year." Then noticing me standing there with his present, he smiled. "Hey, girl, come over and get your Christmas kiss."

The lips I offered to him were numb and cold, and my smile might have been carved out of ice. Hadn't my worse fears just been confirmed? Pam had stayed in touch with Dan all along!

"Merry Christmas!" I babbled, hoping no one noticed the sharp tinge of hysteria in my voice.

"I'll run along and leave you two alone," Chip said. "Two's company, three's a crowd, and all that jazz."

"Actually, I just slipped in here to put something under the tree," I explained as I bent down to put the boxed sweater beneath the lower branches. I don't know why I did what I did next. Maybe I didn't want Dan to see how flustered I was. I do know I wasn't thinking straight as I stood up and slipped my arm through Chip's. "Why don't we go get some punch while Dan plays host?" I suggested, giving him my coyest look from under half-closed lashes. "And I hear you've got a new joke I've been dying to hear!"

I hadn't heard anything of the kind, but Chip always had a joke close at hand. He started telling me one as I led him back toward the dining room. But, to tell the truth, I barely heard a word he said. All I could hear was a nervous ringing in my ears. But I'd be darned if I'd let Dan see how upset I was by the smidgen of conversation I'd overheard.

I could tell by the expectant look Chip flashed

me when we'd reached the dining room that he'd just told me the punch line even though I hadn't heard. "Oh, Chip, that's hysterical! That's just about the funniest joke I've ever heard!" High-pitched laughter spilled from my lips, but way in the back of my throat, I could taste tears. "Quick! Get me to the punch bowl," I insisted, clinging even more tightly to his arm. "After that joke I need a drink!"

If I hadn't known Mrs. Buckley better, I'd have thought there was liquor in the punch. But it was my own nervousness making me so giggly and carefree. I didn't try to calm down, though as long as I kept at this high pitch of gaiety, I knew I wouldn't cry.

I was the belle of the ball, chattering to everyone in sight, dancing and flitting from room to room as if it were my party and not Dan's. All I could think of was keeping my cool and not letting anyone suspect my world was falling apart.

It was after ten, and some kids were starting to say their goodbyes by the time I let Dan capture me alone, and then it was only because I'd blundered into him in the hallway. He caught me in his arms and kissed me before whispering, "Come into the den so I can give you your present."

And then, there I was, face to face in a room alone with the boy who was all I wanted in the world, and I was wishing I were anyplace else. You're crazy, I told myself as I heard Dan saying lightly, "Boy, I thought I'd never get you to myself tonight. You've been a little social butterfly."

I must be really nuts, I thought, avoiding Dan all night instead of trying to be with him. But when I opened my mouth to talk, all I said was, "I figured a good host should mingle with the guests."

He raised his eyebrows, and a shadow swept over his face. "It looked to me like you were doing the mingling," he said. Then, quick as a flash, his usual smile came back. "Let me get your present. It's in the desk."

"Oh, wait!" I wailed. "Yours is in the living room, under the tree. I'll be right back."

I darted out of the room, sneaking into the living room to grab the package from under the tree, then whisking out again before anyone could stop and talk. Dan had looked almost hurt that I'd ignored him all evening, but I hadn't done anything wrong, had I? If Pam had been at the party, I was sure she'd have been all over the place talking to other guys and keeping Dan on his toes. What's good for the goose is good for the gander, I thought grimly as I reentered the den.

As soon as I saw the package in Dan's hands, my heart sank. It wasn't an enormous box—but it was way too big to have just a class ring inside it. I almost hated looking down at Dan's hands, sure of what I'd see. There it was—his ring, right on his finger where it had always been. I had to bite my lip as I handed him his gift. "Merry Christmas, Dan," I said weakly.

"Merry Christmas to you, too, Julie," he said softly, taking my hand and leading me to the couch before handing me the square gold-foil wrapped box tied up with a big red satin ribbon.

Dan was like a little kid, ripping off the wrappings eagerly and exclaiming over his sweater. "Hey, neat! And my favorite color, too! Thanks, honey. I love it." He leaned over and kissed my cheek while I sat like a statue, too limp and disappointed to move.

"Well," he finally prodded, "aren't you going to open yours?"

I felt like throwing it back at him and telling him to save it for Pam. But somehow, my fingers clumsily undid the ribbon and halfheartedly tugged off the foil wrap. "Oh, Arpege!" I managed to murmur, my voice quavering not from happiness but heartache. "And a whole ounce....You shouldn't have spent so much money, Dan."

"I wanted to, Julie." The corners of his mouth turned down, and I knew I'd ruined the whole thing. Why did I always say something stupid?

"Well, it's the nicest present I've ever gotten from anyone." It was true, but that still didn't mean it was what I'd wanted. Seeing his shoulders slump, I didn't blame Dan for being disgusted with me. I tried to pump some enthusiasm into my voice. "I love it, really!"

"Good. I'm glad," he said, but his voice was curt and cool, and I knew he could tell his gift had somehow left me cold. "Well, I'd better go say goodbye to everyone and let you get back to your mad whirl of socializing," he said, standing up and leaving the sweater where it lay on the couch.

I jumped up and linked my arm through his, carefully setting the perfume bottle on the end table. "I'll come with you," I said. "I'd much rather be with you than just gadding about."

"Would you?" he asked, his voice faraway and hollow.

Before I could say another word, the door to the den opened, and Chip popped his head in. "I've been looking for you guys! How about one last dance while Dan says goodbye to his guests, mademoiselle?" he asked, and if I hadn't been so blue, I'd have had to giggle at his idea of a French accent. Well, Dan didn't seem to want to be around me, so...

"You're on!" I said in my perkiest voice, pulling my arm away from Dan's and rushing to the door. "See you later," I called over my shoulder, but I didn't wait for an answer.

"What's wrong with him?" Chip asked as he guided me back into the living room, where a few couples were still dancing. "It's not like Dan to be so grim. Hope he's not afraid you'll fall for my fatal charms."

I was about to say that that was ridiculous. Then I saw Dan standing in the entrance to the room and gave Chip what I thought of as my hundred-volt smile. "Why don't you show me a few of them while we dance?"

"Uh, actually I'm better on the fast numbers." Chip was gazing across the room at Dan, and I knew then he was really afraid Dan might be jealous. So much the better, I thought.

"C'mon." I gave him a little tug. "Let's play Fred Astaire and Ginger Rogers." After that, there wasn't much Chip could do but dance with me, and I made sure he held me good and tight. If Dan thought other guys were interested in me, maybe, but just maybe, I'd have a chance. After all, if I kept him jealous enough, he wouldn't have the time to think too much about Pam, would he?

By the time we were in Dan's car on the way to my house, I'd given him the full treatment, even kissing Chip goodbye under the mistletoe in the front hall.

I didn't want to overdo it, so on the way home I snuggled as close to Dan as I always did. "I wish you hadn't been so busy," I pouted. "Why, do you realize I hardly got to see you all night?"

"You seemed busy enough," he told me, his

voice little and tight. "As a matter of fact, you were so busy with Chip I didn't even think you knew I was there."

"Chip?" I laughed as if he'd said something funny. "Don't be silly. I mean, I like Chip all right, but it's not my fault if he followed me around all night, is it?"

"No, I guess it's not," he admitted, but he still sounded put out.

"Look, Dan," I said slowly as he parked at the curb in front of my house, "remember when you said I had to trust you? Well, that goes both ways, doesn't it? I'm not about to run off with someone else, certainly not Chip Richter. But—well, it's like you said. It's not as if we were going steady, is it?"

I'd hoped that might make him tell me he thought we were, that he wanted us to go together. Instead, his lips tightened into an unsmiling line. "You're free to go out with anyone else you want, Julie," he said in a voice so bleak it made my heart plummet straight to my toes. Everything in me wanted to cry out to Dan that I didn't want anybody else but him, that he was the boy I loved. But I couldn't say it. How could I sacrifice my pride and hold my head up if, after saying all that, I still ended up with Dan coming to me in a week and saying he was back with Pam.

So I just took a deep breath and said lightly, "If I decide to, I'll let you know. In the meantime, I'm having the nicest Christmas ever," I lied.

"You really mean that?" Dan asked, and this time there was no sarcasm in his voice, just something that sounded like hopefulness and made me believe my flirting had worked.

"Do I ever!" For the first time that night, my voice rang with sincerity. Dan's looking at me in that wistful way and the desperate note in his voice made me feel safe and secure.

"Then I guess we don't have to talk about it anymore." And the last thing I saw before I closed my eyes and waited for his kiss was that crooked smile I dreamed about every night.

By the time my parents and Dave reached home, my smile was genuine, and I'd even managed to get excited about my bottle of Arpege. It was a wonderful gift, after all, and as far as Dan's class ring was concerned—he could give it to me anytime, not just at Christmas. And if I could convince him that every other guy in the junior class was after me, why shouldn't that time come sooner and not later?

Chapter Eight

That week between Christmas and New Year's was heaven. Since school was closed for vacation, I didn't have to bear the burden of flirting. And Dan was wonderful, as sweet and thoughtful as if I were the only girl in the world. Maybe if I hadn't heard him telling Chip he'd gotten a card from Pam, I might have even relaxed completely and not always felt that nagging doubt in the back of my mind.

I did try to sound out Dan about Pam one afternoon when we were sitting at Hodie's, our ice skates on the floor of the booth beneath us. Our cheeks were still flushed and icy from spending most of the day on the frozen pond at the outskirts of town, the pond everyone still called Farmer Benton's, even though the Benton family hadn't owned that land since my mom was a girl.

"I guess Pam will be back at school next week." I made my voice as matter-of-fact as possible and popped a french fry into my mouth with what I hoped was a devil-may-care attitude.

"Not until the second day of term," Dan said. "Her dad had to finish up some paper-work in Pittsburgh."

"You mean you've talked to her?" My throat had turned dry as dust, and even the big swallow of root beer I gulped down didn't take the lump out of it.

But Dan just shook his head as casually as if we'd been talking about Maryjo or Mimi or Sue. "Nope. I got a card from her last week, but she didn't say much except that she was feeling a little scared about coming back mid-year."

"Then how did you know she wasn't get-ting here till the second day of term?" I asked hoarsely.

"Her mom called my mom. They're good friends."

"Oh." I pushed the last few french fries around on my plate, ashamed of giving Dan the third degree even as I was thinking snidely to myself that Pam's being "scared" of com-ing back to school was nothing more than a trick to get Dan's sympathy.

Bob Jackson was in the booth behind Dan, and now Dan swiveled around in his seat to answer some question Bob was asking about the swim team. You'd have thought I'd be interested, too, since I'd made the team, but my thoughts wouldn't budge from the subject that kept torturing me.

"So I guess you'll be seeing lots of Pam after she gets back," I said in a tiny voice.

"Why should I?" Dan asked when he'd turned back to me. "Look, Julie, I told you everything was over between Pam and me, didn't I?" He sighed, shaking his head, and I couldn't blame him for being irritated.

"I just meant you'd be seeing her as a friend," I insisted, the lie making my voice sharp and defensive. "I mean, you are still friends, aren't you?"

But if I'd thought I was going to get any information out of Dan, I could forget it. "Sure, I guess so. I don't know. Oh, Bob just reminded me there's a special swim practice Monday afternoon. I'd forgotten all about it." He looked sheepish. "Not very good for a co-captain to forget those things, is it?"

"Guess I'd better practice my jackknife extra hard. We go up against Alton soon, don't we?"

"Three weeks. And all you've got to do is beat them in the girls' dive competitions, and your stardom is guaranteed."

"Don't worry, I'm going to do my best," I assured him. The one thing I knew I did better than Pam Kershaw or almost any other girl at Lincoln High was dive.

Dan became all enthusiastic then and started giving me a co-captain to player pep talk about how great Lincoln High's team could do this year if we all worked our hardest and gave our all. He was so cute as he spoke, his curls waving with every shake of his head, his eyes all crinkly and shining with sincerity. I just let myself sit there and be happy being with him. I'd have plenty of time to worry later.

Monday's practice after school went, as Chip Richter put it, swimmingly. Dan set a new pool record for his butterfly, and the coach promised me that if my dives stayed on the same level, I wouldn't have to worry—I'd be a starter in every meet.

Dan and I swam together in only a few things, so it's only natural my favorite time of all was the free swim at the end of practice. Then, gliding back and forth across the length of the pool like minnows, Dan and I always met at the deep end to grab a quick hug underwater.

This day, Dan was in an especially up and playful mood, probably because of his record-setting swim. I was diving and splashing with him and Chip, enjoying the horseplay too much to even bother flirting with anyone but Dan, wishing this day could go on forever, my happiness sealed like colored crystals in a paperweight. When I saw Chip suddenly stop swimming and pull himself up the side of the pool, I didn't think anything of it. Then I saw Dan start treading water, his eyes not looking at me but watching whatever Chip was doing.

I paddled around so I could see, and what met my eyes made me feel cold all over. It was Pam—and she looked prettier than she ever had, with her golden hair hanging loose except for the plain tortoise-shell barrettes pulling it back on either side of her face and her makeup so carefully put on it looked as if she wasn't wearing any.

My heart was sinking clear down to the bottom of the pool, but I didn't want to swim to the ladder and pull myself out, knowing I'd feel short and squat standing anyplace in the vicinity of Pam while wearing my regulation tank suit. For what seemed like hours, I just stayed where I was, pumping my legs to stay afloat, afraid to turn around and look at Dan. If I saw adoration on his face when he looked at Pam, I knew I couldn't take it.

She didn't even see him at first. Chip was too busy bending her ear, and I could tell by the way she smiled that Chip was being his usual laugh-a-minute self. I felt a shiver go up my spine as I watched Chip's face so glowing and eager, heard his laugh ring out a little too loudly. Couldn't anybody resist Pam's charms?

Pam just stood there, poised as a fashion model, her simple pleated skirt and peach angora sweater making everything in my entire wardrobe seem dull and drab to me. Why had I rolled my eyes when Mom had pointed out a skirt just like that in the Sunday advertising supplement and said I'd look nice in it? I remembered now the way I'd sniffed at it. "Really, Mother," I'd told her, stressing the word Mother to show her how exasperating she was, "no one wears stuff like that anymore."

But I'd been wrong. Pam wore stuff like that, so it was okay. It was more than okay. It was obviously *the* thing to wear.

I had to pull myself over to the side of the pool then. My legs felt too weak to go on treading, my lungs too choked to gasp for air. I did a clumsy breaststroke to the shallow end, when I thought I could slip from the pool and into the dressing room without Pam's noticing. But when I started climbing the steps there, I looked up and saw her head turning in my direction. Then, quickly, with small, graceful steps, she walked away from Chip—heading toward me!

"Hi, Dan!" She called, and the smile that spread across her face made me want to cry. I hadn't realized he'd followed me down the length of the pool until I saw her coming in our direction and felt Dan's hand on the small of my back as he followed me up the fan-shaped stairs that led from the shallow end to poolside.

"Hi, Pam. You know Julie Eaton, don't you?"

Her eyes flicked over me, and her pretty face went blank as a kewpie doll's. Of course she doesn't know me, I wanted to scream.

But I kept silent, and after what seemed like an eternity (it was probably only about four seconds), she nodded seriously as if she'd just plucked my name out of the hundreds who had envied and copied her over the years. "That's right. Julie Eaton. We were in gym class together in ninth grade, weren't we?"

I nodded, not trusting my voice. How well I remembered that gym class! How could I ever forget it when I'd spent most of the year secretly watching her like a spy in the shadows, trying to figure out what she had that made a boy like Dan Buckley interested in her and what I could do to be like her.

"Welcome back, Pam," I murmured through stiff lips, amazed at the normal sound of my own voice. I was suddenly practically stiff with nervousness, but I was trying hard not to show it.

But she'd already forgotten I was there. "We just got in this afternoon," she explained, as if she knew that was what Dan would have wanted to know. "I figured you'd all be at practice." She laughed, a silvery sound that made me think of my own laughter as tinny and unpleasant. "You see, in six months I still haven't forgotten how totally hooked you were on swimming."

"No, I don't guess you would," Dan said,

and, like a radar screen, my ears sensed a certain tension in his tone. "You starting classes tomorrow?"

But before Pam could answer, Chip bustled up, shouting good-naturedly, "C'mon, Buckley, don't monopolize *all* the women! Let's shower and head for Hodie's." He put his arm around Pam's waist as if she were too fragile to face the world with the rest of us. "I'll give Pam a ride," he stated, and I thought he sounded a challenge, as if he expected Dan to tell him he couldn't.

"Sounds all right to me," Dan said slowly, in a way that made me sure he didn't really want to go. But why would he? After all, he couldn't possibly be comfortable with me there. "But it's up to Julie, really," he added, and I was newly aware of his hand resting on my back. Dan was acting all possessive and concerned just to get back at her for leaving him, I thought. He really still loves her. The confirmation of my worst fears was overwhelming.

Somehow I found the strength to shake my head and speak. I even found the energy to turn up the corners of my lips in a smile. "No, you all go ahead. I promised Mom to help her can some winter squash," I lied. "You go with them, Dan," I insisted, refusing to let him see how crushed I was. "You can just drop me at home on the way, if that's all right."

He looked at me strangely, as if I'd spoken

to him in another language. I guessed he was surprised I wanted to take off. I didn't want to go with them because I was so positive I'd already lost. "If that's what you want," he said, sounding puzzled. But the puzzlement, I was certain, was just for show. I wondered if he was working at keeping a note of triumph out of his voice.

"I'll go change," I mumbled, wanting to get away as soon as possible. "Bye, Pam. Bye, Tiger, be a good boy!" I don't know what made me say that to Chip or what made me reach over and give his arm a squeeze. It was just the only thing I could think of to do to cover up my hurt, to look carefree and casual. "I'll meet you in the parking lot," I told Dan cheerfully, using my last surge of spirit to sound upbeat before I trudged wearily to the showers on legs so shaky I wondered if they'd hold me up.

Good old Julie Eaton, I thought bitterly as I stood under the coldest water, trying to numb myself until I wouldn't feel like sobbing. Yep, Julie Eaton, without a care in the world. So what if her boyfriend doesn't care about her and was just passing the time until the girl he loved came back home?

I was terrified that I'd start crying while I pulled on my clothes, and I was proud of my willpower when I didn't. I dressed faster than I'd ever done in my life. It was as if I were playing a crazy little game with myself. If I didn't stop moving, I couldn't think enough to break down and weep. If I made it to the car without crying, I'd be able to keep up my bluff all the way to my house. Good old devil-may-care Julie Eaton, I thought, gritting my teeth against the emotions trying to smother me.

I hugged my books to my chest as I stumbled down the corridor to my locker to get my coat, unpleasantly aware of how puffy I looked in that cocoon of down that had once been my favorite belonging. I held the locker door to steady myself before heading out to the parking lot, then I concentrated on keeping my head high and my shoulders back while I whistled a medley of Bee Gees hits under my breath. And all the time, my mind was repeating, You're almost home, you're almost home.

Dan was waiting in the car for me. I turned on the radio as soon as I got in and made a big show of singing along with it almost all the way home. Anything to avoid a conversation.

We were almost to my house when Dan reached over and turned down the volume. "How come you didn't tell me before that your mother was expecting you?" he asked, and in my ears it rang as an accusation.

I shrugged. "It just slipped my mind. Why?"

"Well, because I'd just figured we'd go have a Coke or something after practice, that's why." Dan sounded a little put out. "I mean, we do usually go to Hodie's after swim practice, Julie."

"Don't let me upset your plans," I said brightly. "You can still go."

He squealed to a stop in front of my house, and I knew he was mad about something, but I couldn't imagine what. After all, I'd have thought he'd be glad to ditch me now. "It's just not the same, Julie. Besides, can't you see how uncomfortable it would make Chip if I went, knowing—"

He paused, and I was sure the words he was biting back were "knowing that I'm still in love with Pam." But what he said was, "knowing Pam and I used to go together?"

"You mean you're not going?" I asked, beginning to see the light.

"Of course not. I'll just go home and do some schoolwork, I guess."

For a split second I felt like telling him it was okay, that I didn't have to help my mom, that we could go to someplace besides Hodie's together, to the Pizza Palace or the Greek coffee shop. But I didn't. Something inside of me just wouldn't stop. My heart was breaking, and I wanted to make things better. But all I said was, "Maybe Mimi Carson needs someone to help her study." I cringed as I heard my own voice, wondering to myself where the words were coming from.

.He didn't even answer. "I'll see you tomorrow," he muttered, staring straight ahead at the twilight that was settling around us, coloring the world as gray and grim as my mood.

"Bye-bye!" I chirped, half-skipping, half-running up the walk, hoping and praying Mom would be out visiting so I could rush to my room and hide my face in my pillow. I knew I couldn't keep up my act any longer. I knew the truth of what I felt would be as easy to read on my face as the big neon sign on top of Hodie's.

And what I felt went as deep and clean into my heart as a stake—Dan was as good as gone. Pam was going to be the girl wearing his Lincoln High School ring. It was only a matter of time, and I had absolutely no control over anything.

Chapter Nine

I wish I could say I'd had the guts to talk the whole thing out with Dan, but I couldn't make myself do it. I was afraid it'd only make things worse. If he was going to break up with me, I told myself, the most I could hope for was to hold onto him as long as possible. The possibility that Pam might not want him anymore entered my mind, but I dismissed it point blank. What girl in her right mind wouldn't want Dan?

Coward that I was, I reverted back to Plan A. I might as well pull out all the stops now to make Dan jealous. I certainly had nothing to lose—and maybe, just maybe, everything to win.

My decision didn't make me feel much better, but at least it coated the pain inside me with a wrapping of numb determination. When I sat down with the rest of the family at dinner, I felt anesthetized, as if I had been given a big shot of Novocaine that numbed me all over.

I was there, and yet I wasn't there at all. Dimly, I could hear Mom and Dad kidding each other about that evening's upcoming bridge party, which was being held at our house. As if through a dense fog, I listened while Dave told Dad about his latest pysch lesson. As if I were a puppet with someone else pulling the strings, my lips formed words and my vocal cords made sounds, as I rushed on overenthusiastically about Lincoln's big swim meet with Alton and how hard we were all practicing for it.

I talked, and I listened, but the tiny black pit inside me knew that none of it mattered, nothing I could say or hear was important anymore. All that mattered was keeping Dan from slipping away, or, if I couldn't do that, letting him go without throwing my wounded pride on the scrap heap as well.

Normally, I'd have been disappointed that Mom and Dad were tied up for the evening and that Dave had shut himself up in his room right after supper to study for a Spanish quiz. But tonight I felt only a sense of blessed relief that I'd be alone.

Alone? It was as if I'd never known the meaning of the word before this. Nothing could get through my dulled, deadened senses. I tried playing my Carly Simon albums but couldn't even remember whose familiar voice was pouring out of the stereo speakers next to my bed. I tried to reread *Catch-22*, but the words swam before my eyes like symbols that had lost any sort of meaning. Finally I just lay flat on my back on the bed, still fully clothed in my slacks and shirt, half asleep, half awake, my mind empty in a way that wasn't particularly pleasant.

When Mom called up the stairs that Maryjo was on the telephone, it was all I could do to drag myself to the extension on the bedside table in their room. I sat with my hand clutching the receiver while I tried to remember how to talk, how to sound cheerful. Suddenly the telephone had a life of its own, like an evil spirit. One day, across those lines, would come Dan's voice, telling me that he and Pam were back together.

I took a breath so deep it made me dizzy. "Hi, Maryjo! What's new?" I asked, waiting with dread for her to mention that Pam was back.

Either Maryjo didn't know yet or couldn't care less. She was too full of her own news. "Tim asked me to wear his class ring!" She was practically screeching with joy. "Isn't that fabulous, Julie? Me, Maryjo McMahon, actually going steady!"

"But I thought you were tired of Tim?"

She laughed. "That's what I kept telling myself. But this year, things changed. You know, ever since he got back from his grandmother's house. I was just kidding myself, putting myself down and telling myself Tim was the best I could do 'cause I was overweight and everything. But since I lost that fifteen pounds, the funniest thing happened. I realized it was Tim I wanted to go out with, whether I was fat or skinny. Isn't that a trip?"

"That's terrific, Maryjo," I mumbled, knowing she was too happy to hear the insincerity in my voice. What would she say if I told her I hadn't even noticed she'd lost weight? Tears sprang to my eyes again as I made excuses and got off the phone. Of course Dan couldn't love me, not when I was such a rotten friend I didn't even notice that my best friend had finally stuck to a diet!

Back in my own room, I sank down once again on the bed, my misery too deep for tears by now. That'll teach me not to be smug, I told myself, squirming at the twisted humor of my life. Here you've been thinking all along how jealous Maryjo must have been of your good fortune with Dan, and what happens? You end up envying her because she's the one who got what you want—a class ring and happiness. It was true, and though I was happy for her, the bubbly quality of Maryjo's voice on the phone had made me feel even flatter.

I didn't see Dan until swim practice the next day, but I knew he'd stuck to his guns and gone straight home after he'd dropped me off, because Sue had walked down the hall with me after third period and said, "Hey, guess who I saw at Hodie's yesterday?"

My heart seemed to stop beating, that's how afraid I was she was going to say she had seen Dan. "Who?" I asked, the word no more than a long breath.

"Chip Richter and Pam Kershaw. And, boy, was he pulling out all the stops to try to impress her! I've never seen Chip come on that strong to anyone. Pam didn't seem to be falling for it, but you couldn't tell. She looked awfully tired." Sue giggled. "Maybe it was the trip from Pittsburgh and not Chip's jokes that were putting her to sleep, though."

"Mmmm," I murmured as if I couldn't care less what Pam Kershaw did or thought or felt. I couldn't figure out why other people, even friends of mine like Maryjo and Sue, just seemed to consider Pam another girl in our class. Was I the only one who was intimidated by her?

"Hey," Sue went on, her eyes all screwed up in concentration behind her glasses, "you think maybe Pam's using Chip to make Dan jealous?"

An icy finger ran down my spine. "Why in the world would Pam being with Chip have anything to do with Dan?" I snapped.

But Sue was so caught up in her analyzing

that she didn't hear the warning bells ringing in my voice. "Oh, just because some people say—" She stopped suddenly, a dull red flush rising on her cheeks, and when she spoke again, her voice was unnaturally high and fast. "Well, after all, Pam and Dan did go together all that time."

"Well, Dan's not going with her now!" I said it so loudly that a couple of freshman girls stared at us and tittered. "Look, I've got to get to class. Maybe Dan and I will see you at Hodie's later," I added pointedly.

I knew what Sue had been about to say, and I hurried off down the corridor as if I could escape from her unspoken words. She'd been about to remark that some people said Dan and Pam were bound to get back together again. I wondered what she'd say if she knew that one of those people was me!

Dan was already in the pool working on his backstroke when I came out of the girls' locker room in my tank suit for practice. He didn't see me, and I stood alone at the side of the pool, watching him, wishing I could get inside his mind and know what he was thinking. But maybe it was better that I couldn't.

When he did climb out of the water, he gave me a quizzical glance, as if he were trying to calculate my mood. I smiled and waved, slipping my hand in his when he came over. He smiled, but it didn't reach his eyes. "We going to Hodie's today," he asked, "or do you have some other plans I don't know about?"

I ignored the belligerence in his voice. Right now I couldn't possibly afford to get into a fight with him. "Hodie's it is!" I said brightly. "I really *am* sorry about yesterday, Dan," I added in a softer tone. "I don't know how I forgot to tell you about having to help Mom. Please don't be mad."

He squeezed my hand, and his face cleared back to its sunny self. "I guess I have been overreacting. It's no big thing, Julie. As a matter of fact, I'm sure it didn't do me any harm to stay home and crack the books."

The coach blew the whistle that signaled the beginning of formal practice then, and Dan and I had no more time to talk. Funny, I'd expected Dan and Chip to act uptight around each other, but from where I was sitting on the bleachers with the girls' diving squad, I could see them fooling around and laughing by the side of the pool when they weren't in the water. If there were any hard feelings between them, they were doing a good job of covering them up.

When practice broke up, I went up to where Dan was standing with Bob Jackson and Chip. They were talking about a new relay they might try, so I stood quietly, not wanting to interrupt. When they stopped, I turned to Dan. "I'll just go dry my hair and change and meet you by the car, all right?"

"You guys going to Hodie's?" Chip asked. Then, without waiting for the obvious answer, he went on, "Guess I'll see you there then. I'm picking up Pam at her house first."

Was it my imagination, or had a shadow of displeasure crossed Dan's features? "How about you?" I asked Bob, leaning toward him in what I hoped was an alluring manner. "Aren't you coming, too?"

He looked surprised that I'd spoken. I'd never talked to Bob about anything but the swim team, and I don't think he'd ever thought of me except as the girl with the good jack-knife dive or Dan Buckley's girlfriend. "I hadn't thought about it," he answered. "I don't know—I've got a math quiz tomorrow."

"Oh, don't be such a grind," I pouted, slanting my eyes at him in a way that let him know I was only teasing. "C'mon, you can give us all a pep talk on how we're going to beat Alton in the big meet."

He grinned then. Anything to do with the swim team, which was Bob's pride and joy, was guaranteed to get his interest. "We'll see," he said, but his eyes were looking at me differently now, as if he were suddenly seeing me as a person, a girl, and not just a diver. "Maybe I'll see you guys there."

"That's more like it." I gave him the warmest

smile I could dredge up out of my cold heart, then batted my eyes at Chip. "We know we don't have to worry about *your* putting studying before fun!"

Dan expelled a long breath through his teeth, and the sound, like air leaking from a steam radiator, was hot and angry. "Look, Julie, we've got one more step of this relay to talk over, so why don't you go get dressed, and I'll meet you in the hall."

"I guess I know when to leave," I said, winking to the other guys, but as I waltzed away, hurt swept over me. Why, Dan had looked almost *disgusted!* Was he already comparing me to Pam and deciding she was the victor?

The weird thing is that, as I pulled on my heavy chino jeans, turtleneck sweater, and pile-lined boots for the trudge through the snow of the parking lot, I felt almost giddy. Not only had I managed to flirt with Bob Jackson—I'd even gotten a response! Dan had to start getting jealous soon when he realized that plenty of other guys at Lincoln would take me out if he weren't in the picture.

When I got to the corridor that led to the parking-lot door, Dan was already waiting, his books in a worn canvas carryall slung over his shoulder, his car keys in his hand. His hair was clustered in damp ringlets around his face, and his posture as he leaned against the wall lockers struck me as weary and defeated.

"You look tired," I told him, trying to keep the concern out of my voice. "Do you think you're pushing yourself too hard at practice, Dan?"

"Now you're starting to sound like Pam." He laughed harshly. "Next thing you know, you'll be telling me to quit the team."

"Quit the team? I'd never do that!" I insisted. "You mean Pam really wanted you to give up swimming? Why, that's the most unfair thing I've ever heard! How could any girl—"

"Let's not start dishing Pam, Julie." Dan's voice as he cut me off had a note of angry command I'd never heard before. It scared me into silence, and for a minute all I could hear was the beating of my heart and the clinking of the car keys as Dan jangled them in his hand. "Well, we'd better get going," he finally said, as if he were forcing out the words. "The guys'll be waiting."

"You should have dried your hair." I spoke as softly as I could so it wouldn't sound too bossy. "You'll catch cold."

"I knew how eager you were to get to Hodie's and see all your friends." The way Dan emphasized the word friends gave it an ugly sound as he turned on his heel and strode out the door.

I had to trot to stay at his heels as he walked rapidly to the car. I couldn't figure out what had gotten into him, but I was afraid to ask. What would I do if he confessed he was edgy because Pam was going to be there with Chip?

Neither of us spoke on the short drive. As a I sat there in my shell of lonely silence, I remembered driving this same way months ago, the day Dan had joked about having mint juleps, and the memory of how happy and peaceful we'd been that afternoon made today seem even more pathetic. How had so much fallen apart since then?

By the time we'd pulled into the lot at Hodie's, I felt meek and solemn. I might have been about to enter a church for a serious occasion instead of a diner full of kids where the rock 'n' roll music from the jukebox speakers sometimes bounced off the walls so loudly it made conversation difficult. I walked up the short flight of steps as if I were on my way to the gallows, wishing we hadn't come here at all.

If Dan was upset about Chip's picking up Pam and bringing her here, no one would have guessed. He gave them both a smile and a big hello, but when Chip asked if we wanted to sit with them, Dan shook his head. "No, Julie and I have something to talk about," he said, and I was afraid those words were my death sentence. I couldn't have been more thrilled than when Bob Jackson walked in right on our heels. Before Dan got a chance to speak, I called Bob's name and waved him over to the table.

With Bob Jackson, luckily, you didn't have to talk about much except swimming, and I was satisfied just to add a few words to whatever he and Dan were discussing. Dan seemed to relax a little when Bob sat down and started talking, but whenever Dan looked at me, I could hear little mental doors slamming. I was so uncomfortable I finally excused myself to go to the girls' room, stopping at almost every other table and booth on the way back, not wanting to give him the chance to start a serious one-to-one conversation with me before we left.

When I did get back to our booth, I sat as close to him as I could and didn't flirt with Bob Jackson. If I showered Dan with affection for the rest of the afternoon, he wouldn't dare break up with me today. He just couldn't!

Chapter Ten

Dan didn't break up with me, and the next couple of weeks I planned a whirlwind of activities, parties, and double dates with Maryjo and Tim for us—anything so we wouldn't be alone long enough for him to start a serious conversation. Not that it did any good as far as my nerves were concerned. Every day made me more and more of a basket case. I spent most of my time in class rehearsing what I'd say if Dan told me he was still with Pam. In one version I took the news calmly and gently wished him happiness. In another, I was haughty and told him it didn't matter to me what he did. In another, I was lighthearted and offhand, assuring him I was glad of the chance to try out my freedom. In reality, I knew I'd be devastated and want to die.

Between classes, I scoured the halls with my eyes, combing the corridors from side to side as if my head were the periscope of a submarine. I was looking for the one sight I didn't want to see—Dan walking with Pam. The only time I did see that, they were walking with Chip, Mike Schultz, Dianne Abbott, and a bunch of other kids, and as far as I could tell, Pam and Dan weren't with each other any more than they were with everyone else. Still, I ducked into a doorway, terrified that if my eyes met Dan's, I'd read signs of his betrayal there.

My grades started slipping, only a little bit, but I wasn't too worried. After all, midterms were still weeks away. But one day Mr. Arnold, my math teacher, stopped me after class and asked if I was having special difficulty grasping the most recent algebraic equations. "I'll work harder," I vowed, ignoring the question since I couldn't even remember what it was we were studying. "Honest, Mr. Arnold, my spot quiz grades will pick up."

"If you'd like special tutoring, Julie, just tell me and we'll arrange something. You're too good a student to get bogged down like this."

"Thank you, Mr. Arnold. I'll let you know," I told him, then dashed from the room, not knowing how to deal with his kindness but not wanting it, either. How could I tell him that in all my personal equations, X was Dan and Y was me, and Pam was the added element that was dividing everything?

Worst of all, I started messing up at swim

practice. Being on the diving board had never fazed me before in my life, but now I felt more vulnerable and alone than ever up there, as if I were on the plank waiting to be judged and sentenced to life or death by a jury of one—pirate Dan Buckley. And when Dan one day made a really minor remark, like, "You'd better tighten up your dives before the meet with Alton, Julie," I shriveled up inside and for the life of me, couldn't think of a snappy retort.

Most of the time I was both numb and frenzied, like the captive ballerina who's told she'll be shot when she stops dancing. I'd turned into a stranger, but a stranger who was still me. I could hear myself laughing too loudly, talking too much, flirting too obviously, but I couldn't stop. If I stopped, I'd think, and right then, I didn't want to think about anything.

My dad always used to say you couldn't avoid death or taxes. I couldn't avoid what I was running from, either, and when Dan just sat behind the wheel of the car one day after school instead of revving the motor and heading for Hodie's, I knew somehow my blackest day had come.

I knew it for sure when he began speaking and avoided meeting my eyes. "I've been wanting to talk to you about something for weeks, Julie," he said quietly, "but it seems we're hardly ever alone together lately."

"Well, there's been so much going on," I began in my new, overbright manner. "There's swim practice and so many parties lately and the basketball games and—"

"Please, Julie," he begged, and he sounded so sad and forlorn that I almost cried for him, even though I knew what was coming. "The more time that's gone by the more clear everything is in my mind."

"What's everything?" I whispered.

"Us, Julie. You and me." He sighed loudly, still staring straight ahead while my eyes were fixed, as if I'd been hypnotized, on his hands, clenching and unclenching the steering wheel.

"What about you and me?" I asked unsteadily.

And then they came, the words I'd been trying so hard to avoid. "I think we should stop seeing each other for a while."

No matter how hard I'd tried to prepare myself for the worst, now that it was happening, I wasn't a good sport or haughty or relieved. I was stunned. And hurt, so hurt I felt like a little ball of nothing but pain. "Why, Dan?" I asked, fighting back the tears that had already welled in my eyes. "Why?"

After an eternity, he answered, "It's just not working, Julie. It's clear to me now that what you really need is your freedom, the space to go out with other guys, to play the field some more. I just don't think we're ready for an exclusive relationship."

That did it. I felt as if I'd been on the rim of a cliff and Dan had just pushed me over the edge. "Don't give me any garbage about 'exclusive relationships,' Dan Buckley," I nearly shouted. "That's some phrase you overheard your mother or father using, and you know it. And don't start handing me a bunch of bull about how I need my freedom. You're the one who wants his freedom."

I was crying now in earnest, and I stopped only to catch my breath before going on. "You've wanted to break up with me for weeks, and I know it."

"I don't know what you're talking about, Julie." His voice was a hollow monotone, his hands still clutched and unclutched the wheel.

"You don't?" I asked, a mean edge sharpening my voice. "I mean Pam Kershaw is what I mean. You've been dying to dump me ever since she moved back to Rockway, and you know it."

"That's ridiculous!" Now he sounded as furious as me. "Pam's got nothing to do with us, so don't go dragging her into this. What kind of creep do you think I am, Julie? Do you expect me to just sit around and do nothing while you throw yourself at every guy in school—even my closest friends? You've been making me look like a fool." He unclenched his hands now and spread them like a lawyer on a Perry Mason rerun pleading his case. "I just can't take it anymore."

"Then don't!" I screeched. "Leave me alone and go back to Pam! See if I care! I don't need you, Dan Buckley!"

I stopped, my own words ringing in my ears. I'd finally said it, I'd finally gone too far. Dan was still staring sightlessly into space, as if some answer waited there. But I knew the only thing that was probably waiting for him that minute was Pam Kershaw, undoubtedly sitting at Hodie's waiting for Dan to ditch me and go to her.

My breath was coming in gasps now, but my tears had dried up in rage. Dan turned to me, his eyes sad and full of regret. But I couldn't stand the tension any longer—the doubts, the worries, everything I'd been feeling. I wheeled around, and out my window I saw Maryjo getting into the new compact car her dad had bought her last month for her birthday. Tim wasn't in sight, and somehow my fevered mind remembered he had basketball practice until late that night.

Without another word, I pulled away from Dan's hand that was reaching for me, fumbled with the door latch, and, grabbing my books and purse with one hand, ran through the slush calling Maryjo's name. I never wanted to see Dan Buckley again as long as I lived.

"Julie, what's wrong?" she exclaimed when I'd hurled myself into the car beside her.

"Please, please take me home, Maryjo," I sobbed.

"What is it? Is it Dan?"

That made me start crying all over again. "I don't want to talk about it now!" I was spilling over with tears and frustration and pain. "Please, I'll tell you when we get home. Right now, just get me out of this parking lot, and I'll never forget it!"

We drove home in silence except for my muffled crying. Then Maryjo pulled up in front of her house. "Mom's in town shopping, I think. Why don't you come in for a minute, Julie?" she asked. "You don't want to go home with your face all splotchy and everything and have your mother asking what's wrong." Maryjo looked concerned, and I knew I had to tell somebody before I burst.

I followed her up the walk and into the house, standing like a department store dummy while she pulled off my parka and threw it down on the little antique chair in the entrance hall. "I'll make us a cup of tea," she said as if I had a nervous breakdown in front of her every day of the week. "You sit on the couch and pull yourself together while I boil the water."

The matter-of-fact way Maryjo was handling my crisis worked, and by the time she came back into the living room carrying a rattan tray with a teapot, sugar bowl, and two mugs on it, I felt a little better.

She poured and fixed the tea, then, setting my cup down on the coffee table in front of me, said, "Now, do you want to talk about it? You might feel better, you know."

This was the opening I'd needed. Finally I could tell someone how miserable I'd been. It came out in a flood. "It's Dan," I blurted. "He's broken up with me!"

"Oh, Julie, no!" Her eyes squinted closed as if she were feeling the full brunt of my pain. "You seemed like such a great couple. Maybe it was just a bad fight," she said hopefully.

"No, it was nothing like that. It wasn't a fight," I went on, sipping my tea to try to still the shaky feeling that was churning up in me. "It's Pam Kershaw. He's still in love with her." There, it was out. I'd finally told someone the awful fear I'd been living with.

"In love with Pam?" She sounded like I'd just assured her the moon was made of green cheese. "But that's impossible, Julie! Dan doesn't seem to care about anyone but you." She sounded totally incredulous. "Julie, is that what he really said—that he's in love with Pam?"

Miserable, I shook my head. "Not exactly. He said he thinks I need my freedom and should start going out with other guys. But I know that's really because he wants to see Pam."

Maryjo looked relieved. "It seems to me

you've gotten yourself into a state over nothing. You *know* he really likes you, and you don't have any reason not to believe that." She was quiet for a moment, and then she said, "You're jealous of Pam, aren't you?"

I shrugged my shoulders and looked away.

"You *are* jealous! I've thought so for a long time. Everytime someone mentions Pam, you get uptight. And whenever Tim and I have been with you and Dan in Hodie's, I've noticed that you practically turn rigid whenever she walks by."

She looked closely at me. "Julie, I don't know what you're so worried about. You're pretty, and you're fun to be with, and you're just as nice as Pam. You've got to stop being jealous. You'll only make yourself—and Dan—crazy."

I knew Maryjo was right. In fact, she wasn't saying anything I hadn't told myself a thousand times before. The rational part of me knew that I was letting this crazy jealousy get the better of me. But whenever Pam's name was mentioned, all the old insecurities came back to crowd out the resolutions I'd made to try and control the jealousy. I didn't know how to overcome it.

I stared at the floor, knowing that Maryjo was watching me, waiting for me to open up to her so she could help. But if I couldn't explain my feelings to myself, how was I going to find the words to explain them to Maryjo?

So I just nodded. "You won't tell anyone about why we broke up, will you? If anyone asks me, I'm just going to say that Dan and I decided together not to get too involved." I covered my face with my hands. "Sooner or later, everyone's going to know the truth anyway, but right now I'd just as soon not be the laughingstock of Lincoln High."

"Don't be silly. Nobody would laugh. But don't worry, I won't say anything to a soul. I don't believe it's over, anyway. Now, let me show you some pictures of Tim and me. Maybe it'll take your mind off things."

I stayed at Maryjo's for another hour, about as long as I would have been at Hodie's with Dan. She was wonderful and almost managed to keep me from thinking about things. Almost.

By the time I got to my house, I was bearing up all right. Nothing mattered to me now but getting good grades and putting up a brave front. I knew that if I directed my misery into those areas, things wouldn't hurt so much.

The next month passed in a haze. I ignored Dan as much as I could, though I always had a glassy smile and a friendly hello for him when we passed in the halls, an effort that left me feeling weak and shaky afterward.

I stopped going to Hodie's. In spite of my story that Dan and I had parted on the best of terms, I couldn't face walking in there without him. Maryjo insisted she'd never seen him there with any other girl, including Pam Kershaw, unless it was at a table full of kids. But that didn't fool me. I was sure they were hanging out someplace together. Even when Maryjo called it to my attention that Dan was looking drawn and unhappy lately, I refused to listen. "It's probably just that Pam's told him she's not ready to get back together with him yet," I told her.

Swim practice was a chore now, all of its pleasure gone. I avoided Dan with as much energy as I'd once watched his every move. It was as if he'd died as far as I was concerned. When he was there, I phased him out and didn't notice him at all. It was only when I got home after school that I'd turn over the images of him in my mind—how he'd looked wearing the green sweater I'd given him for Christmas when I'd bumped into him coming out of science lab; the darling way his curls had fallen over his forehead when I'd caught a glimpse of him bending over the drinking fountain in the morning; the lightning flash of his dimples at practice when he chuckled at some joke of Chip's.

Not even the meet with Alton could lift me out of my doldrums. I placed third in the jackknife competitions, behind two seniors from Alton who, according to the coach, were the best divers in the county. But, without Dan by my side taking pride in my accomplishment, it was an honor as meaningless as all the straight A's I was getting on tests now that I had so much time to study.

Then finally something happened that did snap me out of my stupor. I was walking down the hall, consciously working at looking cheerful and normal in spite of the depression that I wore wrapped around me like a blanket, when I saw a big new poster taped to the hall by the front doors. "Spring Swing," it announced. "Grab your partners for the best March mixer in the history of Lincoln High! Come stag or with a steady, Spring Swing will be ready! Saturday, March 23."

Only two weeks to one of the biggest social events of the school year! Despair sharp as a knife cut into my side as I thought how fabulous it would have been to go with Dan. Now he'd almost certainly take Pam Kershaw. This was the perfect chance for him to flaunt the fact that he'd won her back.

Maybe it was sheer defiance, maybe it was just that I was sick and tired of moping around and wanted my life to get back to something that resembled normal. But then and there I made up my mind that I wasn't going to sit at home in my room crying the night of Spring Swing. I'd wasted enough time flirting with all those guys I'd never been interested in. Now I was going to collect the reward. I was going to go to the dance on some other boy's arm and show Dan he'd never mattered to me at all.

Chapter Eleven

The next day I showed up at school with a new attitude. I was determined to do everything in my power to be more outgoing than ever, anything to make sure the right guy asked me to the Spring Swing.

Because I felt nearly conscious for the first time in ages, I noticed something I should have picked up on before. None of those guys whom I'd thought would be beating down my door when Dan and I split up had asked me for a single date! Maybe it was my fault, I thought, maybe I'd been so wrapped up in my own problems I hadn't projected an open, available image.

From then on, I made myself go out of my way to pick up the threads of my fraying friendships. I also kept a careful watch on who was acting how, which meant keeping track of Pam Kershaw as much as anyone. And I learned two very surprising things.

First of all, I discovered that none of the

guys I'd played the vamp with seemed to have cared. Bob Jackson, I noted, was walking with Lisa Hughes almost every time I saw him, and though he was as warm and nice as ever, it was clear that she was the girl he'd be taking to the Spring Swing. Chip kidded around with me when I approached him one day at swim practice, but when I started trying to lead the conversation around to going someplace for a Coke when we were finished, he mumbled something I didn't hear and dived straight into the deep end of the pool. I was beginning to wonder if I'd turned into some kind of social leper.

The other thing that caught my attention was the fact that Pam Kershaw, now that I felt she'd beaten me and I had no more to fear from her, appeared more and more to me as a real live girl, not some goddess who could get anything she wanted just by being her.

I watched her in the hall once, walking with Mimi Carson, and when I was close behind them, I shamelessly eavesdropped. What I heard filled me with shame—shame at the way I'd misjudged Pam. Mimi was whining about how some girls had given her the cold shoulder when she'd joined them uninvited at lunch, and Pam's voice when she spoke was gentle and hesitant. "I don't think you see how easily you can rub people the wrong way, Mimi," she said. "I know that when you overdo it it's because you're a bundle of nerves, but I think other kids mistake it for being pushy. Try to be a little softer, more mellow."

I slunk away, my eavesdropping making me feel guilty. It was only when I was sitting in English class that the full meaning of what I'd heard hit me. Not only had I been totally wrong when I'd thought Pam kept Mimi around just because Mimi fawned over her so much, I might have been wrong about Mimi, too. Maybe she was just shy and uncertain and acted ridiculous sometimes because she didn't know what else to do. But I'd never bothered to find out, had I? Pam Kershaw had, though. And it was obvious after hearing that snatch of conversation that she was genuinely trying to help Mimi, not to use her as I'd always supposed.

When I saw Pam, a few days after that incident in the hall, standing by the bulletin board reading a notice that listed the parts available for the upcoming spring play, I resolved to say something nice to her, to try to conquer my awful jealousy. This year's show was going to be a comedy, with auditions to be held in three weeks. I'd already decided to try out for one of the smaller roles, just to get back into the swing of things. Now, as I almost bumped into Pam as she stood reading the cast of characters and descriptions, I said, "You should audition for the lead, Pam. You'd be perfect."

She looked at me in surprise, then shook her head and gave a small laugh that rang ruefully in my ears. "Oh, no, I couldn't do that. The girl who gets that role will have to practically carry the whole show. I'm sure they're looking for someone who's got talent and real presence, not someone who'd just look good up there on stage. I sew, you know, so I thought I'd apply for wardrobe mistress."

I was dumbfounded. She meant it, too! I found my voice long enough to make small talk about the auditions before drifting down the corridor in a veil of confusion and shock. This was too much. Pam Kershaw was just as unsure of herself as the rest of us! Maybe even more so, since she worried that no one could see past her pretty face. Well, I hadn't, had I? For the first time, I considered that being desired and accepted for your looks alone might not be all it was cracked up to be. But Pam wasn't getting all sullen and standoffish as I probably would have. Instead, she was willing to work behind the scenes as a wardrobe mistress who'd get none of the glory. It certainly gave me food for thought.

But I couldn't make head or tails of the other thing that was bothering me, and, finally, getting Maryjo all to myself one lunch hour, I steeled myself to bare my soul. "Not a single boy has asked me out since Dan and I split up, Maryjo," I admitted with difficulty.

"I can't figure out why. Is there something wrong with me?"

"No, there's nothing wrong with you, Julie. Don't be silly." But I could tell from the funny look that crossed her face she knew more than she was telling.

"Please tell me what the guys are saying. You must know, Maryjo! I mean, Tim's pretty tight with Chip and Bob Jackson."

"All right, but don't yell at me if you don't like what you hear. Tim said some of the guys mentioned that you'd flirted so outrageously when you were Dan's girlfriend that they're afraid you're just a runaround and don't want to risk getting mixed up with you. And almost everyone is sure you and Dan will get back together again. According to Tim, Dan hasn't shown any interest in any other girl since you two broke up."

A thrill of hope zipped through me but quickly died. "That's just because they don't know that Dan's secretly seeing Pam."

"You don't know that, Julie," Maryjo corrected me, sounding a little annoyed.

I waved the whole subject away with one hand. All I needed was to start getting my hopes up again and I'd really be letting myself in for the big hurt. "What I really wanted to talk about is how to get a date for the Spring Swing. Only a week away, and it doesn't look as if I've got a chance in the world of being invited. And I don't blame the boys for thinking I'm just a tease. I tried to flirt with them when I realized Dan was still hung up on Pam, but I guess it backfired." I shook my head, smiling in spite of the sadness I felt. "Leave it to me to not even be able to do that right!"

"Don't let it get you down." She patted my shoulder absentmindedly, already trying to come up with a solution for my dilemma. "What about Chip? I haven't heard that he's got a date for the dance yet."

But I remembered the way Chip had avoided me when I'd hinted around about getting a Coke after swim practice. I shook my head. "No, not Chip."

"What about Eddie Farrell? He seems interested in you. As a matter of fact, he's sitting across the room right now watching your every move, so don't look up."

For the rest of the day I mulled over the possibility of Eddie Farrell. He was a shy, skinny boy in my math class, brainy and nice, but bashful. I'd guessed early in the year that he had a crush on me by the way he stared at me in class, then reddened whenever I looked his way. Of course, he'd be too shy to approach me himself. But if I made the first move, surely he'd jump at the chance to take me to the Spring Swing.

I'd almost made up my mind to focus all my charm on Eddie the next day. But that night, thinking it over before I went to sleep, I suddenly understood what a selfish thing that would be. If I left Eddie alone, he'd get over his crush and start going out with someone else, someone who really liked him for himself. If I used him just so I'd have a date, he'd think that I was interested in him, too, and I'd end up hurting somebody who'd never done me any harm. I recalled the torture I'd gone through, wondering if Dan was seeing me just to get back at Pam, and I knew I couldn't do that to another human being. No, Eddie Farrell was out of the question. There was only one thing I could do.

The next day I swallowed every last morsel of my pride and went to see Mrs. Blythe in the home ec room. Mrs. Blythe was in charge of the refreshment committee for every big event, and for good reason. The skinny little birdlike woman knew the secret of baking the best cookies and mixing the zingiest punch in Rockway. "I'd like to volunteer to serve refreshments at the Spring Swing," I told her.

I'd only had one semester of Home Ec in ninth grade, but that was enough for Mrs. Blythe to nod her head like a wise little crow and say in her crackly little voice, "Yes, Julie Eaton. Your mother was Peggy Parr, the first of my girls to start gathering ribbons at the state fair."

"Mrs. Blythe, you're amazing!" I said sincerely.

"It's hard to forget a girl as talented as Peggy was," she said modestly. "And if I remember correctly, you made some wonderful ginger-snap cookies for your freshman project."

I nodded to show she was right. "The refreshment committee isn't filled already, is it?" I asked concerned.

"Oh, no, not for this dance. Everyone wants to be chosen, but few wish to serve." She chuckled at her little joke. "But are you sure you want to volunteer, Julie?" I thought I saw sympathy in her eyes. "There's still almost a week to go. I'm sure a pretty girl like you will be asked."

"I'm happy just to man the punch bowl," I said firmly, hoping I sounded more optimistic than I felt. "This year I don't want a date," I fibbed.

"Well, I'm always happy to find girls who are willing to do their share to help," she remarked, "and it's always a pleasure to find someone who really wants to help. I'll put you down for the punch bowl. Be here in the home ec room at six o'clock Saturday night. That's an hour before the dance starts."

"Yes, ma'am." I left feeling more than ever how selfish I'd been. Until Pam had made that remark to me about being wardrobe mistress, I'd always taken for granted that the kids with nothing better to do *deserved* to be stuck with the dirty work. I'd never considered that anyone might deliberately volunteer to help.

Mrs. Blythe's gratitude made me feel less melancholy about working at the refreshment table. I'd accepted the fact that if Dan didn't want me anymore and no other guy in school was going to start asking me out, I was going to have to do something with my life on my own. Maybe everything else was screwed up, but that didn't mean I couldn't do things to help me feel better about myself. If I was more active, more considerate, maybe someday another boy as special as Dan would want to get to know me better. Right now, I doubted it. But at least I'd pulled myself together and decided that anything was better than moping and moaning around.

I did a whole lot of thinking in those days before the dance, and, for the first time in ages, I even confided in my mother. After all, I'd certainly made a mess of my life, so how could I keep thinking I knew so much?

When Dan and I had broken up, Mom couldn't help noticing her daughter didn't have much of anything to do anymore. But, as always, she was tactful and didn't push. She had just asked casually one night, as we were getting dinner ready, "Have you and Dan had a fight, Julie? I notice he hasn't been around much."

"We split up," was all I said that time and every time afterward when she brought up the subject. From the way my lips stayed closed in a tight, thin line, she could guess I didn't want to discuss it.

Right after my talk with Mrs. Blythe, though, I actually sought out Mom in her sewing room. "Busy?" I asked nonchalantly, though anyone with eyes could see she was sitting at the sewing machine stitching up new blue and green plaid curtains for the guest room.

"Not too busy to talk to you, dear," she said, immediately setting down the fabric and looking up.

I sank down on the hassock next to her. "It's about Dan and me." I tried to sound very adult. "We really have broken up for good, and I just wanted to say I hope you won't mind if I don't go to the Junior Prom or anything this year."

Her nose twitched, and at first I was afraid she was going to laugh. But all she did was say, "If you and Dan *have* decided to go your separate ways, why does that mean you'll never have another date, Julie? I'm sure there are other boys in your class who'd like to take you out."

She hit my sore spot there, and my new-found maturity flew right out the window. "No, there aren't, Mom," I wailed, "and it's all my fault! Even if Dan always did like Pam better than me, I acted like a fool. And he was right when he said I made a fool of him as well!"

Then I poured out the whole awful story of my envy and my attempts to make Dan crazy with jealousy. She listened carefully, not interrupting or saying anything until I was through. "So that's the whole story, Mom, and that's why I'm going to have to live with being a wallflower. And now that I've thought it over, I can't even say I think I don't deserve it."

"Don't jump to conclusions so quickly, Julie," she said in her warm, consoling voice. "When you're young, you don't consider the fact that time does heal all wounds and that people do forget. I think you're doing a very brave thing going to the dance by yourself and helping out with the refreshments, and I have a feeling your friends will feel the same way.

"As far as your whirlwind flirting goes," she went on, raising her eyebrows in disapproval, "it certainly wasn't a kind or clever thing to do, but you were scared and not thinking straight. Show everybody that's not what you're really like, and they'll forget all about it. You'll have another boyfriend eventually."

"But I don't want another boyfriend," I protested. "I just want Dan."

"No one gets everything they want in life, Julie. Dan's a person, not a thing. You can't own him or control him or make him feel anything that isn't there. As a matter of fact, maybe if you hadn't tried so hard to hold him, he wouldn't have slipped away."

"What do you mean?"

"Would you ever have been really at peace if you suspected Dan was staying with you only because he was afraid another guy would step in if he were gone?" she asked. She shook her head. "I don't think so. If what Dan really wanted was to be with Pam, he'd have gone back to her sooner or later, dear. Love only matters if that commitment is made freely, fresh every day, if someone is with you because that's exactly where they want to be. If you didn't trust Dan as he was, you never would have."

I couldn't get Mom's words out of my head—maybe because I knew she was right. Dan had accused me of not trusting him, and he'd been right in the long run. Now I saw things might have been different. For the first time, I admitted it might have been my actions and not his undying love for Pam that had pushed him away. And I knew then that if I had it to do all over again, I'd do it all differently.

Maybe I wasn't Pam Kershaw, but did that mean Dan couldn't have been interested in me? Obviously, he had been. And he'd never made me feel as if I was second best. I'd decided that all on my own. I was so sure that he'd decide against me if I gave him time to think that I never stopped flirting or playing games for a minute. It had never occurred to me to just be myself and trust Dan's feelings for me. And maybe by feeling that way, I'd driven him out of my life.

Out of my life and back to Pam? I was sure he'd show up at the dance with her. But now, I knew, I could live with that. After all, I'd never done a single thing to show him I cared. If anything, I'd done everything in my power to show I didn't.

I'd behaved like an idiot. Maybe if I hadn't, Dan still would have broken off with me, but by acting the way I had, I'd guaranteed it. Never again, I vowed, would I make the same mistake. And in the meantime, I was going to have to take my medicine, no matter how bitter it might be.

Chapter Twelve

By Saturday my new resolve was weakening, and I'd have given just about anything not to have to go to the Spring Swing by myself. But I'd given Mrs. Blythe my word, and I was going to stick to it, no matter how unpleasant the evening might be for me.

Luckily, the Spring Swing was a casual affair, so I wouldn't be one of the few girls there not wearing a formal. I'd look just like everyone else—except that I'd be behind the refreshment table at the end of the room, practically broadcasting my datelessness to the entire school.

Since the weather had begun to warm up, I wore one of my favorite lightweight dresses, a blue flowered peasant print in the thinnest wool crepe with a scoop neck and little puffy sleeves, along with my new powder blue ballet slippers, with delicate satin ribbons that wound around my ankles and tied in bows.

Dad offered me a ride, and even Dave said he'd be glad to drop me off at school on his way to pick up Lois, but I said I'd rather use public transportation and would call later if I needed a ride home. I wanted time by myself on the way so I could stay calm.

I almost cried when Mom kissed me good-bye at the door, saying, "You should feel proud of yourself, Julie. Humility isn't a lesson easily learned by anyone. You're doing the right thing." But I just thanked her, then marched off down the street toward the bus stop, her words making it easier for me to hold my head high.

The school was all lit up when I walked over from the bus stop half a block away, and after I'd gone in the front door and left my coat, scarf, and gloves in my locker, I walked by the gym on my way to the home ec room in the basement. The chaperons were already there, along with kids from the decorations committee, who were adding some last-minute crepe-paper streamers to the hanging garlands and tacking the crepe-paper skirt on the refreshment table. On the bandstand, the Rockway Rockers, the school rock band, were busy setting up their instruments and plugging in their amplifiers.

It all made me feel sad and deserted, more alone than ever, and if my feet had won, they'd have made a mad dash back to the bus stop and the safety of home. But my head ruled for a change, and I went down the stairs to help Mrs. Blythe.

"Thank goodness you're here, Julie!" Mrs. Blythe greeted me when I walked in, running her fingers through her short gray hair in a harried way. "Two of our girls got last-minute dates and cancelled, so I'm afraid we're terribly shorthanded. If you hadn't shown, I'd have been in a real pickle."

That made me thankful I hadn't chickened out. Giving Mrs. Blythe a businesslike smile, as if the idea of playing truant had never crossed my mind, I got right to work, helping two shy tenth-grade girls, so bashful they were both practically twitching when they weren't whispering and giggling together, arrange the homemade cookies on big tinfoil-covered platters while Mrs. Blythe went back to mixing the punch in big soup cauldrons.

"When you girls are finished, cover the trays with more foil and then take them upstairs to the refreshment table. We'll take two trays up and leave two trays at the ready down here. One of the boys from the decorations group will be down in a minute to take these pots of punch upstairs. I'll be in charge of filling up the punchbowl, so all you girls will have to do is make sure we don't run out of napkins and paper plates and keep the cookie trays looking presentable." She gave her instructions in an efficient manner, sounding a little like my idea of an army top sergeant, then went back to her mixing.

I helped Carole and Kim, the two tenth-graders, with the cookie trays, then took my place behind the table, unwrapping packages of paper plates and napkins. A few of the guys in the band I knew slightly looked my way in amazement, as if they couldn't believe I was actually here as a committee member and not a dancer. But I acted as if I were doing the most normal thing in the world, and instead of pretending I didn't see them, I made myself smile and call, "Want the pick of the cookies before the crowd arrives?" And when they came over, I rearranged the gaps they made on the trays as if serving cookies was what I'd been born to do.

Of course, I felt more ill at ease when kids started pouring into the gym and the band began to play. Some girls were openmouthed in shock when they saw me at my lowly station, while a couple of the guys I'd flirted with so shamelessly looked embarrassed and pretended they hadn't noticed me as they led their dates onto the dance floor. The nerve, I thought at first. As if I'd actually cared if they ever asked me out. Then I saw it from their perspective and understood why they were acting skittish. I'd come on to them, so how could they know a date with them wasn't the most important thing in the world to me?

Maryjo and Tim arrived about half an hour

after the dance had started, and from the way they were holding hands and sneaking a kiss when the chaperons were turned the other way, I could see that Maryjo had finally fallen for him hook, line, and sinker. She looked fantastic, in peach slacks and a ruffled satin top to match, both of which showed off her new, slender figure. And once again, she came through for me in the friendship department, leaving Tim for a bit to come chat with me.

"Only one cookie!" she said merrily. "This time I'm not going to have to get rid of my new wardrobe."

"You look great, Maryjo," I assured. "And thin as a reed."

"You don't look so bad yourself. Better watch out, or you'll be too busy dancing with the stag line to refill the cookie platters."

"Not me." I shook my head firmly. "I'm here to do a job, and that's all I plan to do."

"Well, just between you and me, I think you deserve the Purple Heart. I can imagine how hard it was for you to do this."

I shrugged. "Somebody had to." Then, in case she might think I didn't appreciate her support, I added, "But thanks for the praise. My ego needs all the help it can get these days."

She winked as she turned away. "Don't worry. You're going to be A-okay."

I was getting more apprehensive by the

minute, though. My eyes were glued to the door whenever I wasn't actually busy serving or filling, awaiting with dread the entrance of Dan and Pam.

Mimi Carson sashayed over with, of all people, Eddie Farrell. I hoped she wouldn't be too hard on him. "I never thought I'd see the day when you'd deign to patrol the punchbowl," she said snippily. "My, my, does this mean that if you can't have Dan Buckley, no one else is good enough?"

A snide comeback was on my lips, but then I remembered that snatch of conversation between Mimi and Pam I'd overheard. As levelly as possible, I answered, "To be honest, no one else asked me, Mimi. And I figured since I go to this school, I may as well do my bit to help."

Funny, but my words made her face soften at once, and her voice had lost that challenging, brittle tone when she said, "Yeah, maybe you're right. I never thought of it that way." She smiled, and this time she looked less hard, almost pretty. "I guess I should think about helping out sometime myself." Then, as if she were going to whisper a state secret, she leaned over and murmured, "And, don't worry, Julie, I won't tell anybody you weren't asked for a date."

I looked up quickly to see if she was being sarcastic, but the look on her face was totally innocent, and I realized with a jolt that, just by not losing my temper with her and letting her get my goat, I'd won Mimi over as some kind of ally.

I hadn't even had time to get over that shock when I got the next one, perhaps the biggest one of my entire sixteen years. Chip Richter entered the gym, and the girl his arm was protectively circling was Pam Kershaw!

They came straight to the refreshment table. "Wow, trying to find a parking space near the door tonight is like rush-hour traffic on the Loop in Chicago!" Chip exclaimed. "Hit me with some of that joy juice, beautiful."

Pam laughed wildly as if he'd said the funniest thing in the world, and when I glanced over and saw the way she was gazing up at him through her giggles, I could tell she was in love. Pam Kershaw was in love—and not with Dan Buckley!

I was so paralyzed by my discovery that Mrs. Blythe had to reach over and take the ladle and paper cups from my hands. "Just help them with the cookies, Julie," she suggested as she dipped out their punch.

I guess it's true that surprise can be blinding, because until Pam bent to examine the cookies, I hadn't even noticed that she was wearing a very special accessory with her white angora camisole top and pale blue wool skirt—a Lincoln High School ring around her neck.

"You're going steady?" I croaked.

"Chip finally asked me to wear it last night," she said, her face aglow. "I thought he *never* would!"

"But—but I didn't even know you were going out," I stammered.

"You know me, king of the Secret Whirlwind Romances," Chip kidded. Then, in a more serious tone, he added, "If this dingbat's father hadn't decided to pack up and go to Pittsburgh, she'd have had my ring long ago."

"You were going out before this?" I asked weakly.

"Just a few times before we moved," Pam explained. "Chip was so busy being cool I didn't even know he liked me until I moved back." She laughed, then flashed him a look of affection. "And here I'd been pining away in Pennsylvania thinking some other girl would have snatched him away before Dad got transferred back here."

"Never, baby," he assured her, his hand resting on her shoulder as if that was the only place it was meant to be. "I'd have waited forever for you—or at least until summer."

She rolled her eyes at me. "It's not easy going steady with a comedian."

"Congratulations!" I said warmly. "I think it's wonderful." And then, to my amazement, I leaned over and kissed her on the cheek.

"Thank you, Julie," she said warmly, her

face still wreathed in smiles. "And thanks for the cookies, too. We'll be back."

"She just doesn't want to eat too much before I start twirling her around the floor," Chip told me, leading her toward the dance floor as if she were the most fragile china doll.

Oh, boy, have I ever been a fool, I thought when the full impact of what they'd said had sunk in. Dan and Pam really *had* broken up before her father's transfer! He must have known all along that she'd been seeing Chip since her return. And if I'd only talked to him, maybe he'd have told me that. But, no, I was too busy playing stupid games and punishing myself with comparisons to Pam to even have noticed that she and Chip seemed genuinely interested in each other.

As the absolute stupidity of my treatment of Dan sank in, so did dizziness. I might have fainted if Mrs. Blythe hadn't noticed. "You look a little peaked, Julie," she said kindly."Why don't you take a little break and have some punch and cookies downstairs? We'll be all right without you for a few minutes."

Was I ever thankful for the chance to escape! My mind was spinning and reeling in confusion. But even as I sat on a chair in the home ec room and sipped my punch, I knew the fact that Pam was wearing Chip's ring wasn't going to change things for me. I'd blown it but good.

I rested a bit, then trudged back up the

stairs, just marking time now until the evening was over. My worst fears hadn't come true, but what *had* happened hadn't exactly made me feel like singing.

"I can take over the punch bowl now, Mrs. Blythe," I told her when I'd returned. "You look as if you could use a bit of rest yourself."

"Bless you, dear. I must say I wouldn't mind putting my feet up for ten minutes or so. Just send one of the other girls down to fetch me if there's a problem."

After that, I was so busy I didn't have time to think or mull over what I'd done. As a matter of fact, I was so occupied I didn't even notice Dan come in until I looked up and there he was, standing at the table.

When I looked at him, my mouth went dry as cotton, and I could feel my heartbeat speed up. I had to wet my lips before I could even speak. "Hello, Dan," I said as naturally as I could, "would you like some punch?"

"Sure," he said, friendly as ever, acting as if we hadn't been avoiding each other like the plague for weeks. "That sounds good."

I ladled out a paper cup full, my eyes skimming the room as I did it, trying to figure out who he'd come with.

"Would you like a cup for your date?"

He smiled, just enough for one dimple to form. "Oh, I haven't got a date tonight."

"You don't?" I gulped, then not daring to say anything more, started busily straightening the rows of cookies on the tray nearest me.

"No, the girl I was planning to ask had other plans."

My heart fell to my toes with a thud. After all I'd been through, was he torturing me by telling me he *was* still hung up on Pam? Or was there another girl already? "Next time you'll have to ask her before she gets another date." I was trying to sound chummy and cheery, but the words came out all flat and muffled, and I was afraid if he didn't leave soon, I'd lose all self-control.

Instead, he just kept talking in that maddeningly casual way, as if we were discussing the weather and not the fact that he didn't care about me anymore. "Oh, no, she didn't have another date."

"Oh," I mumbled.

"No, I saw her name on the refreshment committee list, so I figured the only way I'd get to see her at all was to come here by myself."

The cookie I'd been about to rearrange tumbled from my fingers. "Dan?" I whispered. "Dan?"

When I lifted my head to look at him, a single tear was already trickling down my cheek. Ever so lightly, his fingers brushed it away. And now his smile, the two-dimpled one, told me everything I wanted to hear.

"Do you have time for a dance, Julie?" he asked quietly.

With the most beautiful timing that made me her slave forever, Mrs. Blythe picked just that instant to pop back up. "Mrs. Blythe," I asked, my voice strangled and giddy, "would it be all right if I took a break for just one dance?"

"Of course, Julie. We don't want your young man to think I'm a tyrant, do we?" She chuckled, and I hugged her, then walked away to join Dan on the other side of the table, my feet about five feet off the ground. Even her old-fashioned terms didn't irritate me, because *my* young man was exactly what I wanted Dan to be.

It was a slow song, and we didn't talk at all. We just—well, we just *were*. Dan's arms were around me, and I could feel his warm breath in my ear, and I wanted to stay there forever and forever and ever. That's how happy I was.

When the song ended, Dan took my hand and led me out to the hallway. "But, Dan," I asked, "what's happened? I thought you hated me."

"Don't be silly, Julie. How could I ever hate you?" he asked, his hand tipping my face up for his kiss.

"But—but I was so unfair, so horrid!"

"Yes, you were," he said seriously, then chuckled. "And I wasn't exactly Mr. Cool myself. I was so hurt and furious when you accused me of still being after Pam that I couldn't think straight. All that talk about trust, and you didn't even trust me when I said our relationship had ended!

"And I was pretty ticked off about the way you were going after other guys, too. Then, after we stopped seeing each other, I noticed that your big flirt act stopped, too. Finally, it sank in that maybe you were making eyes at everyone else only because you really did think all the time I was still interested in Pam. And the more I thought about it, the more I didn't blame you. I mean, I'd never even bothered to tell you that Pam was dating Chip—and not me—when she left."

"Oh, Dan if you knew how miserable I've been! It's been horrid! And I thought I was so smart trying to make you jealous!"

"You don't have to make me jealous, Julie. You never did. From the time I first started really noticing you at Green Hills, I never thought about anybody else. And when I found out you loved to swim as much as I did, I knew I'd finally met the girl for me!"

"You mean Pam doesn't like swimming?" I vaguely remembered him making some vague comment once about Pam and swimming, but I couldn't remember what it was.

He grinned. "Talk about jealous! She was jealous of the way I love the water, and there's no way to fight that. I hope Chip knows what he's letting himself in for. She won't be happy as long as he's gung ho for the team."

"Oh, I think Pam's special enough that the right boy might be able to overlook that," I said, feeling old and wise for a change.

But Dan just chuckled and shook his head. "Do my ears deceive me, or do I hear praise for Pam Kershaw coming from you, Julie Eaton?"

I smiled. "Boy, I really was awful, wasn't I? I never even gave Pam a chance. Now that I have, I like her. I can understand why you went out with her for so long."

He gave me a long, searching look. "You're not afraid you might convince me of how wonderful she is?"

"I'm not worried anymore, Dan. Honest. You already know how wonderful Pam is, and if you'd rather be with her or anybody else than me, there's not much I can do about it, is there?"

He took my hand and squeezed it. "You've done a lot of growing up lately, haven't you? How would you like to give it another try, Julie? No ties, no binds. We'll just take it day by day and see what happens."

"I'd like that," I whispered. "Oh, Dan, I'd like that very much! And I promise I'll always trust you. *Always.*"

He grinned crookedly. "Do you trust me to not step on your feet during the next dance?" he asked lightly, pulling me gently back toward the lights and music of the gym.

"Well, I wouldn't go *that* far!" I laughed,

eagerly keeping step with him, ready to join the dance again, a dance that might have been a special celebration just for me. Finally, after all the pain and confusion, I had a feeling everything was really and truly going to be all right. How could I ever have wasted so much time worrying over whether Dan was going to give me this ring or if he'd lose interest in me one day? Looking back, I couldn't believe how easily I'd let my own happiness slip through my fingers.

Never again, I vowed silently as Dan led me out onto the dance foor. Maryjo caught my eye and winked, and I grinned back happily. From now on, I knew I was going to be happy enough just being me.